I0619911

HIGH ON BIGFOOT

ARMAND ROSAMILIA

SEVEREDPRESS

HIGH ON BIGFOOT

Copyright © 2023 Armand Rosamilia

WWW.SEVEREDPRESS.COM

ISBN: 978-1-922861-64-1

CHAPTER ONE

Buck knew this was a mistake, and yet he'd decided a summer in the mountains, with his best friend, while growing and smoking weed might be interesting.

"There will be no smoking of the product," Gestapo Karl had yelled as soon as they were all together, sixteen newbies, all from Los Angeles, San Francisco or even San Diego, all taking the long drive to the middle of nowhere to make some money.

You had to know a guy in order to get this summer gig, and Buck's best bud Aiden's dad had worked up here for most of his life. Until the motorcycle accident last year. Now he'd handed it off to his only son to continue the legacy.

"Bro, my great grandfather used to work with the original dudes who started this," Aiden had said. He was driving his beat-up Volkswagen bus, which Buck thought was such a cliche. Without his own ride, though, Buck never said anything to his friend.

Instead, they drove into the mountains. This would be Aiden's second summer and Buck's first, and they were excited about doing something important before they had to go to community college or find a real job.

This was their summer, and they were going to spend it getting paid and high.

Aiden listened to awful music, though. Crap his old man loved, like Led Zeppelin, Pink Floyd, The Doors and Grateful Dead. Old people music.

"Can't we put on something cool?" Buck had asked.

"This is cool. Pass me that." Aiden took the joint and inhaled deeply. "This skunkweed is nothing. Wait until you smoke some real, fresh stuff. Not this oregano."

Buck now wished the drive had been longer, because Gestapo Karl seemed to be looking right at him as he shouted commands and told them what they could or couldn't do.

Most of it was what they could not do.

"Only males allowed on the mountain," Gestapo Karl shouted. "If anyone tries to smuggle up a female, they will not only be fired... but sent to the cave. Do we have an understanding, ladies?"

Buck knew he was going to pay for it, but he raised his hand anyway.

Gestapo Karl snickered. "This ain't high school, you stupid idiot. What?"

"What's the cave?"

Buck thought the guy was going to explode, spit flying from his mouth, his bald head turning such a bright red it was nearly going back to white, the blood throbbing.

Gestapo Karl took a deep breath and he stopped shaking. He pointed a meaty hand at Buck. "Trust me, you don't want to ever find out. We've lost a few men over the years. Never mind me sending you to meet your maker, son... he'll find you if you're bad."

Buck glanced at Aiden, who motioned with his hand to shut up.

"No alcohol, either. If I smell it on your breath, you're fired. If you queers diddle with one another's little peckers, you're also gone. No females means you touch yourself in private and no one hears or knows about it," Gestapo Karl shouted. He was pacing now. "You sixteen won't make it through the first month. Likely not even the first week. This is hard, rewarding work, like our ancestors did before the government tried to stop us."

Gestapo Karl ranted for the next ten minutes about cash crops and government conspiracies and whatnot. Buck couldn't care less. He was here to make money. He got high but it wasn't his life, like it was Aiden's. His bud wasn't happy unless he was rolling a joint, smoking a joint or talking about rolling and smoking his next joint.

"There are over a hundred men working on this mountain. Some of you will be assigned specific duties, like guards. Others will work to harvest. Some will be inside making food or running errands." Gestapo Karl stared at Buck. "Others will be on latrine duty. We need to keep the area clean of our presence. If Johnny Law raids us, there needs to be nothing they can find that says we were here."

Buck groaned inside. He knew he was getting latrine duty, and this summer was going to be a bust. *So much for the great outdoors and being one with nature*, he thought.

CHAPTER TWO

"Tell me about this cave," Buck asked Aiden as they trudged through an endless field of marijuana plants.

Aiden grabbed Buck by the arm and pulled him closer. "Shut up, idiot. You don't talk about it in public. Keep it to yourself. Jeez, bro."

Buck had been assigned to latrine duty, and since Aiden seemed to be his friend, he was given the same awful job. Aiden was not happy.

Neither was Buck. He'd asked an innocent question and gotten the worst job you could get. The other dozen or so hired men were snickering behind his back and staying as far away from him as possible, as if even talking to him would get Gestapo Karl riled up and they'd suffer the same fate.

"I got us the worst job in camp," Buck said. "I might as well know the answer to the question."

They arrived at the latrine, which was nothing more than a series of fenced off spaces, using old fences and a hole dug in the ground, with a large industrial bucket at the bottom. A rope snaked up out of the hole and could be pulled up to empty the bucket.

"Do they aim for the rope?" Aiden groaned.

It smelled awful. Even covering his nose, Buck could taste the stench. From the look of the fencing, they also aimed there, too.

"Gestapo Karl said we haul them out, three times a day, and walk the bucket down the mountain to a specific spot he gives us each day, and dump them." Aiden looked like he was crying. "We put lime or whatever is in the bags over there into each hole to clear the stench so the animals don't search it out, bro." Aiden glanced at Buck. "Especially anything living in the cave."

Buck groaned. "Stop messing with me. Tell me about the cave."

"Nope. Man, you screwed me out of a good summer of getting high and working on my muscles," Aiden said.

Buck glanced into one of the holes and nearly puked. "It looks like you'll get a good workout carrying buckets of crap down the mountain."

Aiden was in Buck's face so quickly, Buck nearly fell into one of the holes.

"No, bro, I won't be hauling buckets. You will. I didn't get us in trouble, and I didn't ask a dumb question. I got this duty because of you, and it sucks," Aiden said, jabbing his finger into Buck's chest. "You are going to do the bucket duty and I'll do the cleanup and dump stuff into the holes. Got it?"

Buck had never seen his friend so angry, and it was scary. Aiden was usually high and cool. Chill.

"You haven't smoked in hours," Buck said quietly. "You're stone cold sober."

"I'm not happy." Aiden jabbed his finger once more before turning away. "I knew it was a mistake to bring you."

Buck was hurt. They'd been friends forever. They'd hardly ever fought, and it was usually over dumb things that meant nothing like toys or baseball. Aiden was a Dodgers fan and Buck loved the Angels. That's about as far as it got. Until today.

"I'm sorry," Buck said quietly. "Maybe I'll go and talk to Karl."

"No." Aiden was waving his hands. "That's the worst thing you can do. He'll fire you. He only wants a couple of guys up here that are new. He'll toss you off the mountain and I'll go with you. I need this money. I'm saving to buy my own organization. In the future, I'll have this setup on a mountaintop, bro. You can come and work for me."

Buck thought Aiden was crazy. It was one thing working for an illegal marijuana harvester, but running your own? That was nuts. It was only a matter of time before you were caught and sent to prison.

Besides, pot was legal in so many states now. It was only a matter of time before everyone could find a doctor to get their own medical card and not have to buy from some hood in a back alley. Aiden's dream would've been great a few years ago.

"I just want to make some money and buy a car," Buck said.

"We need to get to work." Aiden pointed at a hole. "Grab and haul it down. He told you where it was supposed to go."

Buck wasn't afraid of heights but he knew he'd have to hug the side of a precipice and dump the buckets, with the potential to slip and fall highly likely.

With my luck, I'll go over and the bucket will cover me in crap, Buck thought. *They'll find my dead body covered in excrement.*

Buck took a bucket and marched down the trail, trying to remember where he was supposed to go. He'd been so annoyed when he'd learned he was getting latrine duty he'd half-listened to the instructions.

A few workers were seated near the cabins and they laughed when they saw him, waving their hands in front of their faces.

"That dude ain't staying in the cabin with us tonight," one of them said as Buck passed. "He can take ten showers but he'll still stink."

Buck thought about the cave and whatever lived in it. Maybe they had mountain lions or bears. He wasn't sure what kind of wildlife was up here with them. He knew he should've done some homework first, but he'd been too busy doing nothing until it was time to leave.

He hated Aiden right now. He wondered if the rest of the crew would treat him badly, and if he would take it out on Buck.

The trail sloped down, past the work areas, and Buck had to duck and fight branches to get to the designated spot. He thought Gestapo Karl had said it changed every day. Buck wondered if anyone would even notice if he dumped the buckets in the same spot over and over.

Buck found the spot and looked out at a beautiful sight, rolling hills below and a crisp, clear sky. This was heaven.

Except for the smell from the bucket, which he dumped.

He took one last look and sighed. There were a dozen buckets to carry here today, and he supposed they'd fill up quickly, especially after meals.

Maybe I'll try to be positive, Buck thought. *I'm getting paid. In the great outdoors. I'll never see this sight again, probably for the rest of my life.*

Buck turned and jumped, nearly falling off the mountain.

There was someone watching him. He got a glimpse for only a second, but he was sure there was a big, shadowy figure to his right, through the dense brush.

Buck kept an eye out as he walked back to the latrine. He only felt eyes on him but didn't see anything.

CHAPTER THREE

Buck and Aiden were only allowed one shower each, and only five minutes to rinse off the stench that clung to their clothing and bodies.

Gestapo Karl timed it on his stopwatch in front of the entire camp, who watched the two as they showered, clapping and shouting.

"You both still stink," Gestapo Karl said. He turned to the crowd. "Should we give them another three minutes?"

"No," was the resounding answer from the crowd.

Gestapo Karl shrugged his shoulders and showed his teeth. "Oh well, boys, looks like this is as good as it will get for you. You might want to burn your clothes and boots."

"When can we wash our clothes?" Buck asked.

Everyone stopped talking and Gestapo Karl spat some tobacco juice on the ground, inches from Buck's bare feet.

"We don't worry about that stuff. Do you think we have a laundromat up here, idiot? You find a stream and see what you can do, but do it on your own time." Gestapo Karl turned and waved his hand over his head. "Time to eat, peasants. Second shift needs to be ready to go in an hour, before the sun drops over your dainty little heads."

As Gestapo Karl walked off, a smile plastered on his face, Aiden punched Buck in the arm. Very hard. "Thanks for getting us in trouble."

"Trouble? I asked a question. I guess I'm not allowed to do that," Buck said. He wanted to punch Aiden back but knew his friend was angry and would likely attack him.

Aiden stalked back to their cabin, shaking his head, wearing only a towel.

Buck followed. The sun was dropping and it was getting cooler.

Once inside the cabin, Buck saw that all of his belongings were scattered across the floor, mixed in with Aiden's stuff.

"Thanks," Aiden said through gritted teeth. Buck sighed and began picking up his things, while everyone in the cabin held back laughter.

We should leave. Cut our losses, Buck thought. *Before there's actual trouble.*

Buck found a set of clothing and got dressed. He knew he still smelt.

"You two need to find another place to sleep," someone from the back said. "You smell like crap."

There were a few chuckles but no one openly confronted either of them.

Aiden, now also dressed, grabbed his things and headed toward the door.

"Where are you going?" Buck asked.

"To sleep in my bus." Aiden was out the door and Buck wondered what he should do.

The next comment answered it for him. "Looks like his boyfriend left him. He can't stay here. That much I know."

Buck took his things and stepped outside. The night was so calm, only rustling in the upper branches. He'd never seen so many stars over his head, either.

Aiden was a shadow walking down the dirt road, heading to his vehicle, which was down at the bottom of the mountain. It would take at least an hour to get down there. Buck didn't want to follow and then be told by Aiden he wasn't allowed.

Buck looked back at the cabin. He heard some laughing inside.

Unsure what to do, he put his back to the side of the cabin, trying to get comfortable on the wooden porch. There were no chairs and he'd left his blanket and pillow inside. He knew better than to go back in.

This is not what I thought it would be, Buck thought.

He closed his eyes and tried to relax, but knew he wasn't going to get any sleep tonight. He'd also skipped dinner, which meant he wouldn't eat until breakfast tomorrow.

Buck didn't want to cry.

"Hey, what are you doing? No one is allowed to be outside after dark." It was a man Buck didn't know, but he carried a rifle and shined a flashlight beam in his face. "Get inside."

Buck knew better than to explain why he was out here. The guy likely already knew anyway.

"Fine," Buck said, shielding his eyes from the light. He got up, grabbed his things and went back inside the cabin.

No one was inside. They'd all gone out the other door to dinner.

Buck worried they'd mess with him when they came back. He moved his blanket and pillow to the far corner, where a couple of the bunks looked damaged and no one was using them.

His stomach growled.

Screw this. I need to eat, Buck thought and tried to hide his stuff in the corner, between the bed and the wall.

He went to the mess hall and got in line. No one messed with him, but he knew better than to try to sit next to anyone. He found a small table toward the back and sat down.

Buck was nearly done with his watery mashed potatoes and uncooked green beans and whatever they were trying to pass off for meat when a smaller man sat down across from him and gave a quick nod.

The man looked Mexican or Cuban. Buck didn't know. Maybe he couldn't speak English.

"Do you want my green beans?" The man was staring at Buck and spoke with a bit of a Spanish accent.

"Uh, no thanks. I don't even want mine."

The man smiled. "Then can I have your green beans?"

Buck lifted his plate and the man slid the green beans onto his plate and said something in Spanish Buck hoped was a thank you.

"Don't worry about these guys. Someone else will step up and do something stupid soon enough." He smiled, showing his jagged teeth. "I'm Mario."

"Buck."

"Two years ago I did latrine duty. It was not pleasant, but the boss won't keep you over there the entire season… if you stop asking questions," Mario said.

"Understood." Buck knew he needed to keep his head down and do the job. "How many years have you been doing this?"

Mario shrugged. "Five years on this mountain. Before that I worked in the jungles in South America for a cartel. Meth lab."

"Wow," Buck said.

Mario laughed and slapped the table. "You white boys are so gullible. I worked at McDonalds in San Diego growing up. My buddy dragged me up here to work but then he disappeared."

Buck laughed and shook his head. "You got me."

They ate for a couple of minutes.

Buck kept opening his mouth but didn't say anything.

"What? You can ask me questions," Mario said.

"When you say your buddy disappeared…"

Mario shrugged again. "There's something on the mountain. Gestapo Karl wasn't joking about it, either. No one goes out at night. Not unless you're well-armed."

"I thought there was a crew that worked nights."

Mario nodded. "They work inside the far buildings. Prepping the marijuana."

"Okay, I get it."

Mario put his hand up. "Seriously. Do not go out at night, and try to have someone with you at all times if you do. It is not safe."

CHAPTER FOUR

The walk to the bus was ridiculously long, and Aiden kept tripping on loose rocks as he picked up speed going down.

He stopped and got his breath after nearly falling for the tenth time, hands on knees and panting.

A twig snapped somewhere to his right, deep in the woods.

Probably a squirrel or bird, Aiden thought. He hoped that's all it was.

The urban legend of a monster roaming this mountain, looking for lone hikers or workers, came back to him, and he turned to look back the way he'd come. Was it too far to hike back up and slip into the cabin, or was he better off to keep heading down and sleep in his bus for the night?

Buck had ruined everything by being... well, by being Buck. Too many questions. Too curious for his own good.

Aiden wondered why he'd invited him this summer. They were friends but he should have known this would push it too far, Buck would get under his skin and everyone else's skin.

I'm going to lose a lot of money because of him, and I'll never get my own distillery, Aiden thought. His goal was to work in one of the local distilleries back home and learn the business. Then, with the money he'd saved and the profit from the pot he sold, he could buy his own.

Aiden stopped and groaned.

Dispensary, not distillery. Weed, not alcohol, you moron, he thought.

Another twig snapped, this one even closer.

It was too dark to see what was out there, and every dark shadow looked like a monster to Aiden. He hadn't been high in too long now, and the world was becoming clearer. He didn't like it.

Living his life in a drug-haze meant nothing touched him, nothing bothered him. No one could put him down now and crush his feelings.

A slight breeze brought a stench that made Aiden cover his nose.

As a kid he'd come across a dead skunk in his backyard, and the smell made him puke. It was something he'd never really forgotten, and his stomach roiled with the memory of it, never mind the smell that he'd caught on the wind.

Then it was gone. Aiden peered into the darkness but he didn't see anything out there except the shadows of trees.

Like whatever was there, the dread that pulsed from it, had walked away.

Aiden shook his head. *Man, I need to get high. This is nuts. I'm like a little kid out here*, he thought.

He wished there was a way to drive his bus up to the cabin to sleep. He felt exposed down here. While there might not be monsters following him, there could definitely be law enforcement.

Aiden's father had told him about a raid years ago, when fifty armed officers had swarmed the site and beaten everyone. They destroyed the crops, the buildings and slashed the tires of everyone so no one could escape.

The actual owners of the marijuana were never on property, though, and they hadn't even skipped a growing season before they found a new spot on the mountain.

There were endless acres to hide out here, and Aiden remembered last year when another group had tried to start up too close to where they were.

Gestapo Karl had led a large group with rifles and torches. Aiden had heard the gunshots like everyone else who'd stayed behind, and saw flashes of a small fire in the distance.

They'd burned down the rival's crops and the rumor was there were bodies buried or given to whatever dwelled in the cave.

Maybe that's what followed me down the mountain, Aiden thought. *It had a taste for flesh now.*

Aiden knew, if there really was a beast living on the mountain, it had a taste of human meat a long time ago.

He hoped he was small enough to not be tempting, even as a snack.

Aiden also hoped he had some weed in the bus to roll and enjoy.

Of course, if Gestapo Karl or anyone else smelled it on him, he'd be immediately fired. If he had weed stashed he'd need to smoke it all as soon as possible so he wasn't caught.

He was in sight of a vehicle, but as he got closer in the dark he saw it wasn't his precious bus.

All of the vehicles had been spread out over a couple of miles at the base of the mountain, away from any paths going up.

Aiden wondered how the compound received supplies, since it would be such a nightmare to have to carry everything up.

There were a couple of four-wheelers parked next to Gestapo Karl's cabin. That was likely the way they brought up the bad food and water, as well as seeds and whatever else was needed.

Aiden wanted to learn the business but knew he'd never figure it out working here. No one was interested in teaching anyone the business for fear they'd start their own mountainous weed farm.

He wondered if he could trust Buck with helping him out. Maybe he could recruit him to keep his eyes and ears open so they could pool their earnings from this summer and then start their own distillery.

Dispensary, dammit, Aiden thought.

He knew he was kidding himself. Buck had gotten them in trouble, and they'd learn the inner workings of the latrine area and nothing more. So much for his big dreams.

Another twig snapped but it seemed farther away. Aiden took it for a good sign.

Maybe he could find his bus and have a nice, peaceful sleep.

He didn't understand why he'd even walked all the way down here. Was it because he was mad at Buck, or was he afraid the others in the cabin would attack him?

Aiden kept walking, seeing vehicles at times but none of them his bus. He had no flashlight and had to rely on the moonlight, which made it slow going. There was no actual path so he was crashing through underbrush and nearly banging into trees every few feet.

He heard a vehicle approaching and saw a headlight, crouching down.

"Where are you, idiot? This is dangerous for all of us," a man shouted.

There were two headlights and Aiden could see two men on each, all carrying rifles.

"Hey, don't shoot. I'm here," Aiden said. He put his hands up and stepped out so they could see him.

Aiden had heard another couple of branches snap in the woods, not far from where he was.

I'll take my chances with these guys, Aiden thought.

CHAPTER FIVE

Mario walked Buck back into the cabin and nodded at a few of the other Hispanic workers, who nodded back.

"You're safe with us, but you'll need to recognize that," Mario said to Buck, showing him to a top bunk over where he slept. The guy who'd been up there hopped off and moved his stuff to an empty bed.

"I do and I appreciate it," Buck said.

Mario shook his head. "No. That's not what I'm saying." He rubbed his fingers together. "We need to get paid."

Buck nodded slowly. Mario wasn't helping him out of kindness, out of helping the weak member of the herd. He was doing it for his own personal gain, and Buck had fallen for it.

"So… you want me to pay you not to bully me, and to make sure no one else does it, either?" Buck asked. He'd put his bag on the top bunk but thought he should grab it and find another bed. Take his chances, knowing he'd made himself a target.

"I'm here to help." Mario smiled. "We can put together a payment plan, if you'd like. You won't need money on this mountain."

Buck tried not to show fear but knew he was failing. "I'll need it when we're done working, though."

"Every week we get an envelope of cash. Everyone gets about the same. I'll need to sit down with you and take my cut. Is that understood?" Mario was staring at Buck.

Buck knew at least half of his money was going to be taken, if not more. He'd be working for nothing. At this rate, he could've gotten a job at a fast food place close to his house and made more money.

What can I do, though? Trying to talk to Gestapo Karl might make me an even bigger target. He might even be the mastermind of this scheme, too, Buck thought.

"Okay. Fine." Buck climbed onto the top bunk and prayed no one messed with him tonight.

Mario chuckled. "It will be great doing business with you, new friend. No one will go near you again."

Buck wondered if he refused what Mario would do. He'd seen the military movie where everyone in the platoon put a lock in a sock and hit the weakest man until he cried.

I'm the weakest link, Buck thought.

He didn't want to cry and fought it for the next hour, wiping his eyes and trying not to make a sound.

Buck sat up and scanned the room, a few minutes before lights out. Where was Aiden? Had he really wandered all the way down the mountain to his bus?

He noticed there were a couple of other men, fighting not to cry, on the top bunks on either side of him. They'd obviously also been suckered into Mario's shakedown.

Buck tried to fall asleep but failed, jumping at every noise, real or imagined. He was waiting for a beating or for someone to steal his bag.

Had Aiden made it to the bus? Buck thought he should've gone with him. It would be safer taking his chances in the damn woods.

Buck saw Aiden wander in with a couple of other men right before the sun came up, and Aiden looked tired.

Aiden fell into the closest empty bed and the two men both leaned over and whispered something to him, but it was too dark to see a reaction now he was out of the moonlight streaming in from the windows above them.

I wonder why there are no windows at a normal level, so we could see outside, Buck thought.

He supposed it was because of not only the police sneaking through and seeing what was inside, but also the animals on the mountain.

Buck wondered what exactly was on this mountain, because there was an underlying fear. When Mario was sucking Buck into being friends, he wasn't lying when he'd said not to go out alone at night.

It might be why Aiden was back, because he'd been caught outside alone.

Buck was scared. They had a lot of time left to work, and it had only been a few hours, really, since they'd arrived. The work was going to be hard, made harder by Mario and his crew.

Gestapo Karl might not be the worst thing up here, either.

Maybe Aiden will want to leave, Buck thought.

Buck saw it lightening outside and knew any minute now the calls would be made for everyone to rise, get dressed, get food and get to work.

As soon as they made the call, Buck was out of bed and already dressed. He slipped on his boots and rushed to see Aiden.

The line out the door to the latrine was already long, and Buck knew he'd have a lot of work to do today.

Gross, he thought.

He got in line when he didn't see Aiden, washed his hands and went to get some breakfast.

Buck got some food and water and went to sit down next to Aiden but Mario shook his head and pointed at a table, where half a dozen others were seated. "You sit there. That way I can protect you from thugs."

By the look on the other men's faces, they'd been suckered like Buck and were also paying protection.

Mario sat at a table next to them, watching and smiling. "Starting tomorrow, girls, you'll each hand over one item per meal. Got it? Enjoy all of your food today."

Buck was ashamed to nod his head along with the others.

How am I going to get out of this? I can't do this all summer, Buck thought.

He couldn't see Aiden from where he was sitting.

Buck hurried up and ate and was heading toward the door when Mario intercepted him.

"What?" Buck asked.

"I don't like the way you stare at me, bro. I'm not like that, so stop staring at me like a piece of meat." Mario got in Buck's face. "I could easily walk away and let the animals get you. Remember that."

Buck didn't think Mario was talking about the actual animals in the woods.

"I'm not like that," Buck said.

"You better not be. Got it? If I find out you and your boyfriend you came in with are actual boyfriends…" Mario ran his thumb across his throat.

Buck wanted to laugh because it was so cliche, but he put his eyes down and made sure not to make contact with Mario.

"Go clean the latrine," Mario said and walked away with a chuckle.

CHAPTER SIX

They worked in silence for nearly an hour before Buck couldn't take it anymore.

"What happened to you, Aiden?"

At first, Aiden didn't answer Buck.

"I tried to go to the bus. They stopped me. End of story," Aiden said.

"That's it?" Buck moved out of the stall he was working in when a man pushed past him and began unbuckling his jeans. "Jeez, dude, gimme a second."

The man grinned. "Feel free to stay as long as you want, but the smell might knock you out."

Buck rushed to the stall next to Aiden. "Seriously, what happened? I thought the monster on the mountain got you." He chuckled until he saw Aiden, at his stall door, staring at him. Very angry.

"What does that mean, Buck?"

"Nothing. A joke," Buck said. "I just want to know what happened to you."

Aiden sighed. "I got down to where the cars were hidden but then some goons on three-wheelers found me and dragged me back. Gestapo Karl had to be told and he was not happy being woken up in the middle of the night. He said I'll be doing latrine duty the entire summer."

Buck hid his expression, and he felt bad for it, but he almost smiled. If Aiden was told he'd be doing this the entire summer, it meant, as long as Buck kept his head down and his mouth shut, he might get to do other things.

Aiden was staring at Buck. "Wipe that stupid grin off your face. I know what you're thinking."

"No, you don't."

"Yes, I do. You're thinking, if you stop acting like an idiot, you'll get to do something other than latrine duty, leaving me here to rot," Aiden said.

Buck shrugged. "Fine. Maybe."

"Definitely. Jerk." Aiden turned his back and began raking the trench to keep it flowing. "It doesn't matter, because you can't keep your mouth shut. You'll ask more questions and annoy Gestapo Karl."

Buck hoped Aiden was wrong.

"I think I have some weed on the bus. I might sneak out again, in a couple of nights, and get high. I can't take this," Aiden said quietly. "Are you coming?"

"No. I don't want to do this for the summer. Besides… I think I have some trouble," Buck said.

Aiden smiled. "Mario and his protection racket? Yeah, newbies always fall for it."

Buck sighed in relief. "Fall for it? That means it isn't real."

Aiden stopped and shook his head. "Oh, no. It is dead real. Mario isn't playing around. I'm surprised he didn't tell you about the newbie from last summer who refused to pay him and his crew."

Buck swallowed. "What happened?"

"Rumor is they dragged him up to the cave and tied him to a tree. Never heard from the guy again."

"No way is that true," Buck said, but he was more than a little worried.

Aiden shrugged. "Believe what you want to believe. All I know is, I need to keep out of the way of everyone and do my job. Get paid."

"Get paid your full paycheck, while this guy takes part of my money."

Aiden shrugged again. "Get back to work. I don't want to be caught talking, and you might have a way out of this yet."

"What if I went to Gestapo Karl about Mario?" Buck asked.

Aiden shook his head. "This has been going on for many years. It's a kickback to Gestapo Karl. Do you really think he doesn't know? I hear his only rule is not letting it go past the first year. To weed out the weak, the complainers."

Buck sighed. "Then I'm screwed."

"For this summer you are. I had to do it. Hell, my old man had to pay for his first year, too. Everyone does," Aiden said. "Just get it over with and next year come back and get your full pay."

Buck wanted to punch Aiden. "Why didn't you tell me?"

"Because then you wouldn't have wanted to come. Am I right?"

"Yes," Buck admitted. "Still… it would've been nice to warn me."

More men were using the other stalls and it was beginning to really stink.

Buck went back to work, mad.

How was any of this possible? Definitely not legal, Buck thought.

He chuckled. *None* of this was legal. They were on a mountain, growing marijuana. The Feds could raid them at any moment, and they'd all go to jail. Prison. He'd have a record. Ruin the rest of his life.

For what? Less than what he'd been promised, too. Mario and his crew were going to get rich, while he'd go home and still be poor. None of this was fair.

At lunchtime, Gestapo Karl shook his head and grinned at Buck and Aiden. "You eat outside. You both stink. I'll send some food out."

Buck and Aiden sat down on one of the benches and waited.

"I bet we don't eat," Buck said. He was hungry, tired and stunk. He wondered what would happen if he quit. If he'd even be allowed to walk away from this illegal operation.

Mario and two of his crew walked out with two plates of food.

Lunch was a double cheeseburger and tater tots, which Mario began eating in front of them.

Aiden stood up, fists balled.

Mario took a big bite of cheeseburger and dropped it back onto the tray. "Relax, bro. I just wanted to make sure no one tried to poison your food. I remember you from last summer. You still have that chip on your shoulder, which might get you in trouble with some of the less savory types up here."

His two buddies were laughing.

"I think you also need protection," Mario said, dropping the food tray onto the ground. The guy holding the other tray did the same.

"I paid my dues last year," Aiden said.

Mario shook his head. "No. I don't remember that. Is there any way you have a receipt you can show me?"

His crew was laughing again.

Aiden sat back down on the bench and glanced at Buck, angry.

This isn't my fault, Buck thought, but kept his mouth shut.

"You'll also be paying us this summer," Mario said. "Do you have a problem with that?"

At first Buck thought Aiden was going to get up and fight, his hands still wrapped into fists.

"No," Aiden said quietly.

Mario and his hyena disciples walked away and Buck took a look around before picking his tray up off the ground. Luckily, most of the food was still intact.

Aiden had already wandered off.

CHAPTER SEVEN

"I'm not giving Mario any of my money," Aiden said for the hundredth time that afternoon.

Buck kept his mouth shut, because if he agreed or argued the point, Aiden turned his venom on his friend.

"I guess we can't tell Gestapo Karl about it," Buck said.

Aiden turned on his friend, nearly hitting him with the rake he was using in the latrine. "Who do you think gets a kickback on this scam, huh? I bet Gestapo Karl started this."

Buck shrugged. "There's not much we can do, though. Unless we tell on them and get fired, we have no other choice but to pay it."

"I already paid it. Last year. We need a plan," Aiden said.

"A plan?" Buck was excited and scared at the same time. The thought of not having to pay the extortion was a good thing, but he knew it would be highly unlikely they'd get Mario to back off without some bloodshed.

Mostly Buck and Aiden's blood would be shed, he knew.

"We need to lure Mario and his friends to the cave and let the monster eat them," Aiden said, staring into the latrine pit. "Unless we can find weapons and kill them, but that's too risky. If anyone finds their bodies we might be in real trouble."

Buck sighed. "Why would we be in trouble?"

"Because everyone knows what everyone else is doing up here, that's why. Because if Mario is in with Gestapo

Karl, he'll know what just happened. Because they can't call the police on murderers, they'll take care of it themselves." Aiden was still staring into the latrine hole. "They'll drag us up the mountain to the cave."

"There isn't a monster up there," Buck said quietly. He had no idea but wanted to assure himself. "If there was, someone would've spotted it by now. Gestapo Karl would've rounded up a group with shotguns and they would go and kill it. Right?"

Aiden shook his head. "Gestapo Karl is scared of it. You can tell. Everyone is. As long as no one gets caught outside at night, the creature doesn't bother with us. They toss fruit and vegetables and sometimes raw meat up the trail to appease it each year."

Buck thought of being out in the woods by himself and feeling watched. "This is ridiculous. We're going to get a monster from a cave to kill someone for us. Do you hear how crazy that sounds?"

"Keep your voice down," Aiden said. Two men walked into the latrine to do their business. "Forget everything you know. Everything you've ever been taught. There is something up there."

"And what if there isn't? What if it's a tall tale so no one will get out of line?" Buck asked.

Aiden shook his head. "My father saw it."

"I don't believe you," Buck said, but by the look on his friend's face he didn't think he was lying. Aiden really believed there was a monster in a cave on the top of the mountain.

"Well, my father isn't a liar. He saw it years ago, while chasing after a couple of the goats they used to use."

Aiden sighed. "They stopped using farm animals because they'd end up being lost. Killed. Scattered bones on the trail, as if the creature was letting you know it wanted more… or you'd be next."

"This is stupid." Buck nodded to the two men as they left, but they both ignored him. "Even if we wanted to, how could we lure Mario's men up there, anyway?"

"I'll figure out a plan. You need to follow along. Got it?" Aiden began raking the latrine again. "We stay out of the way. We do our jobs. With any luck, before our next envelope of cash, I have it all under control."

Buck doubted any of this was going to work out but he didn't have his own plan. Might as well at least hear Aiden out and see what he came up with.

"Sure," Buck finally said. With nothing else to say, the two friends went back to work.

Gestapo Karl walked into the latrine area and shook his head. "It stinks in here."

Instead of pointing out the obvious, that it was a latrine, both boys kept their mouths shut and kept working.

Gestapo Karl laughed. "Relax, soldiers. I'm messing with you. So far you're doing a good job. Only a few days into the season, so you have more than enough time to screw this up."

Buck kept his head down and kept working, not knowing what was happening. Why was Gestapo Karl suddenly being nice to them? It seemed like a setup.

"Thank you, Sir," Aiden said as he kept working.

Gestapo Karl was pacing back and forth behind them. "Attention to detail. That's what I like."

Two men walked in and stopped when they saw Gestapo Karl.

"Get lost. Either hold it or find a bucket," Gestapo Karl barked at the two men, who ran off. He chuckled. "It's so much fun having power. Not that you two will ever know, but still… sometimes things work themselves out, even for losers."

Buck tensed up but kept raking the dirt.

"I have a new assignment for one of you," Gestapo Karl said.

Buck glanced at Aiden.

"Only one. You two work it out. After dinner one of you will meet me at my cabin." Gestapo Karl walked out without another word.

Buck counted to twenty in his head, making sure the man was gone before he turned to Aiden. "What is going on? I thought you said this was going to be fun. We'd earn a lot of money. Build muscle. Smoke some weed."

Aiden frowned. "Can't you ever think for yourself? I'm sick of carrying you all the time."

"Don't be a jerk," Buck said. He knew this was going to be his last summer working on the mountain, and wondered if his friendship with Aiden could last. "Feel free to go to his cabin after dinner."

"Why? Do you think you deserve it?" Aiden asked. "I've been here longer. I'm not the one screwing up and getting us into trouble."

Buck shook his head. "No. I'm saying I won't argue or fight with you. Enjoy whatever it is."

Aiden threw down his rake. "What do you know about it?"

Buck was confused. He stared at Aiden.

"Is this a setup? Are you trying to make me look back?"

Buck sighed. "I know as much as you do, which isn't much. Nothing, in fact. I'm agreeing with you that you earned whatever this is. You've been here longer. You brought me in. I get it. Whatever it is… I hope you get whatever you're asking for."

Aiden was inches from Buck's face now, spit flying. "What does that mean? I should kick your ass."

Buck shrugged. He still had the rake in hand and would use it if need be. He was sick of being pushed around.

Has this always been our relationship? Aiden bullying me, getting angry for no reason, being a jerk? I think it has, and me being such a loser and not having friends made him the only one I really hung out with, Buck thought.

Buck took a step back and kept working, worrying they'd be caught arguing and not doing what they were supposed to do. He needed to figure out how many more days of this torture he had to go through before he could go home.

CHAPTER EIGHT

"It's up here somewhere. They said to follow the path," Billy said.

"There isn't a path. I'm going back." His brother, Clay, wanted to get back to work. They'd been sent halfway up the mountain to scout for stray plants and to make sure no one was spying on them. No unknown footprints. No trail cameras set up by the Feds.

Billy shook his head. "Stop being such a baby. We've been up here for six years and you and I both know the rumors."

"Yeah. There's a monster up here with a taste for human flesh," Clay said.

Billy laughed. His brother was always going to be an idiot. "No. I don't think so. Remember when we were kids and Mama always swore there was a monster in her closet? Remember what happened?"

Clay nodded. "That's where she hid the Christmas presents."

"Exactly." Billy snapped his fingers. "It's the same thing here."

Clay looked past his brother. "You think there are Christmas presents in the cave?"

Billy groaned. "No. I think there really isn't a monster. The cave is where they hide the really good weed. Maybe all the money they make. Who can say? It might be filled with expensive champagne and the good food only the bigwigs get to have at night, while we eat the grub food."

"I thought the burgers last night were really good," Clay said. "I even had a double cheeseburger."

"Well, once we find out what's in the cave, we'll be able to buy triple cheeseburgers and fries that aren't overcooked," Billy said. "Keep an eye out for anything. The cave has to be around here somewhere. Keep an ear out, too, because we don't want to be caught."

Billy knew getting caught meant they'd be kicked off the mountain. Or worse. He'd heard the rumors over the years of people going missing, and knew it wasn't because of a creature living up here. It was because they saw what they weren't supposed to see.

A cave filled with treasures.

"How will we get it out of the cave, if there really are bottles of wine and steaks?" Clay asked.

Billy laughed. "I don't know if it's wine and steak, although that would be really nice. It might be a treasure chest filled with gold coins. I heard pirates used these mountains to hide their booty."

Clay didn't know if that made sense, since they were far from the Pacific Ocean and he doubted pirates would carry heavy chests all the way up here.

"See? Here's a clearing. I bet we're close," Billy said.

Clay joined his brother and looked up. The trees crowded in above but they had a big space without anything growing. The soil was dark but there were pieces of something white poking through here and there.

"What's that?" Clay bent down and dug out some dirt with his fingers. He fell back. "That's a bone."

Billy bent down and chuckled. "Yeah. Maybe a squirrel or a hedgehog. Look how small the bones are."

"But not all of them," Clay said, pointing at what looked like a much larger bone. He wondered if it was human. He hoped not.

"Nah. The bigger ones are horses and cows," Billy said.

"They don't look like horse bones. They look like people bones."

Billy helped his brother back to his feet and smiled. "These aren't even real. Look how white they are. These are props put here by the pirates or Gestapo Karl to scare us off. And you fell for it, Clay. Come on. There's no way you're this easily turned away from real treasure."

"No. Uh, yes…" Clay was confused. Billy always talked really fast and said weird things to confuse him, like he was doing now.

"Keep up. We're almost there," Billy said and started to walk across the clearing to a break in the underbrush on the other side.

Clay tried to keep up but Billy kept holding onto branches too long and letting them slap Clay in the face. Billy thought it was really funny by the way he kept laughing each time.

They'd been steadily rising as they moved, and Clay's calves hurt. He wasn't used to so much actual movement, preferring to sit around all day smoking weed. No physical things if he could help it. They'd make enough each summer on the mountain to live the rest of the year in their shared trailer. Sell enough weed they'd purchased to get by, too.

"Slow down," Clay whined as Billy got ahead of him. He could barely make out where his brother was now.

Clay was nearly running as he realized Billy might leave him behind just to be cruel. He worried he'd be lost on the mountain, and it would get dark soon. There was nowhere to hide, nothing to eat or drink.

Billy would play dumb, too, if he made it back by himself. Claim Clay must've run off down the mountain. He'd never admit to leading Clay up here.

"Hey, wait up, Billy. This ain't funny," Clay yelled.

"Shut up," Billy said, inches from Clay, popping out from behind a tree. "You want the camp to know we're up here, or the monster to know we came for his treasure?"

"No," Clay admitted. Billy had scared him and he thought he might've peed himself a little.

"Then try to keep up already. You're so slow we might have to sleep up here or risk falling off the mountain at night." Billy grinned and patted his brother on the back.

"Maybe we should go back," Clay said.

"No way. We're so close. I can feel it." Billy turned and started walking again, Clay struggling to keep up.

"What if it isn't what you think it is, bro?" Clay was falling behind and needed to take a break. His legs hurt and he could barely breathe the higher they rose up the mountain. "Slow down."

Clay couldn't see Billy anymore, and he wanted to run back down the mountain and return to work. Pretend none of this was happening, whatever this actually was. As if they could be so lucky to find a treasure.

"Seriously, you're getting me mad now. Where are you?" Clay was struggling on the thin trail, and thought he was off it now. The branches kept slapping him in the face and the roots were tripping him up.

He stopped to take another breath, hoping to hear Billy. All he heard was his own heartbeat and panting.

Clay kept going, knowing it was a mistake. Knowing nothing good was going to come of this, as always. They'd be escorted from the camp and told never to return. The few days they'd already worked would be for no pay since they'd broken the rules.

The trail was up ahead, a wide path.

Clay stepped onto it and followed, seeing what had to be the cave ahead.

"Billy? Where are you?" Clay got within ten feet of the cave mouth, a wide crack in the side of the mountain, and stopped.

It stunk.

Clay thought a dead squirrel or racoon was around. Maybe even a skunk. He turned full circle and gasped when he saw Billy.

He had been eviscerated, his body ripped open and lying on a thick tree stump. Intestines were piled next to his dead body.

Clay turned to run and figured out where the bad smell was coming from.

It stood at least two feet taller than Clay, with shaggy mottled hair and smelled so bad it made Clay gag.

The eyes, big and red, were the last things Clay saw before a massive paw swung through the air and sliced easily through his neck.

CHAPTER NINE

"We need to find these two idiots before they're lost or another crew finds them," Gestapo Karl said to Mario. "Worse, the damn government is creeping around again and grabs them. You know Billy and Clay are too stupid to keep their mouths shut. They'll lead the Feds right to us."

Mario shook his head. "They're dead by now. It'll be dark soon. I say they left. Got tired of the hard, honest work."

Gestapo Karl smiled thinly. "Honest work? That's funny. No, they wouldn't leave. They're too stupid to pack it in quietly and run away. They went looking for trouble and maybe trouble found them, if you know what I mean."

Mario nodded. "I can't risk anyone going out there, though. They'll end up gone, too. Chalk Billy and Clay up as two more missing. Maybe it will get the rest of them in line."

"Or it will scare them off. We haven't had anyone genuinely go missing for a couple-three years," Mario said. "Maybe it's beginning again. Maybe they got too close…"

Gestapo Karl put his hand up and frowned. "Don't say it. We do what we need to do each year, right? We feed it. Make sure it stays up there and never comes down to hunt. Doesn't have to, either. That thing has it good and has for more years than I can remember."

"Eventually it will die, though, right?"

Gestapo Karl shrugged. "Maybe. It's been alive for decades. The indigenous people from the area talk about it. Taking their livestock and children. Hundreds of dogs have gone missing over the years. We made a deal with it."

"Does the thing know a deal is still in place?" Mario asked.

Gestapo Karl groaned. "I don't know, you idiot, I haven't had a cup of coffee with it. Never hung out in the cave and let it show me his art."

"It does art?"

Gestapo Karl wanted to smack Mario in the face, knock some sense into him. As muscle and an extorter of the newer members of the crew, he was great. Not a smart guy, though. A definite follower. He'd do just about anything Karl said, but he needed everything explaining to him.

"Take a few guys, well-armed and well-lit, up the trail and find them," Gestapo Karl said and stared at Mario. "Did I stutter? Did I blink?"

"No, sir," Mario said. "But, uh… I don't want to risk my own men. The ones loyal to me."

Gestapo Karl smacked Mario in the head, knocking the smaller man to the ground.

"Loyal to who?"

Mario stayed on the ground. "You, sir. Come on, you know what I meant. The guys who follow my orders, handed down from you."

"Don't forget that, or you'll be part of the yearly offering up the mountain. Got it? I've made too much progress over the years I've been trapped on this rock.

Too much is also at stake, and I have bosses to report to. If the government got involved, if a stupid girlfriend or parent wanted to find Billy or Clay and came snooping around… we'd all be in trouble."

"I understand," Mario said and slowly got back to his feet.

"No, I don't think you do. If we were arrested, you'd sing like a bird and get four to ten, tops. I'm running this operation on the ground, so I'll go down for life. Even though it's legal to sell our product in this country, we don't go through those channels. I'm not paying tariffs and taxes and having to modify our strains and all that garbage." Gestapo Karl sighed. "Before morning, those two idiots need to be found. Hell, I don't care if you have to shoot them in the head to get them to come back to camp."

"We'd lose two good workers," Mario said.

Gestapo Karl chuckled. "No, we wouldn't. They're both lazy and slow. If you can get them back, have them take over for the newer morons doing latrine duty."

Mario smiled. "I'll take those two with me. They won't be missed. Two young punks thinking they could make a fortune working here. I don't like their attitudes."

Gestapo Karl nodded. He didn't really care who Mario took. None of them were irreplaceable. Even Mario. Karl could find another bully amongst the crews and set up the same deal with him.

"I don't care who you take, I just want it done. Now. Go," Gestapo Karl said.

Mario nodded and rushed out of the cabin.

I need this to go away so we can get back to work, Karl thought.

He knew he only had a few days until some of the bosses would arrive to inspect this year's crops and make sure everything was running smoothly.

The air was cool tonight, with a slight breeze Karl had felt when Mario had left. Despite the time of night and the fear of being outside and exposed, he couldn't help it.

Karl stepped out and took in the perfect air, redolent with the smell of soil, trees and plants, and an underlying taste of the marijuana being grown.

After all these years, he'd thought the smell of the pot plants would be so ingrained he'd forget they were there. His nostrils and brain constantly filled with it. Karl was wrong. He still got the tingle, still knew when a strain was getting ready to be harvested.

Karl had worked on the mountain long enough to know how to do this job, and tried to surround himself with the proper people to do it correctly.

His bosses had never been disappointed. They'd given him large bonuses, and his pay wasn't too shabby. Add in the money taken by Mario from the newbies, and Karl was set for life.

Back home in Los Angeles, he had a wife and two kids. His beautiful wife knew what he did for a living. She helped out when he was home for a few weeks at a time, helping him to sell it street-level. Karl skimmed enough product each growing season to keep him not only high with a private stock, but he had enough to sell to friends and family.

His daughters would be going to high school this year, and he'd need to make sure he had more than enough for college for them.

Karl's nest egg grew all the time. He'd made sure his bosses dropped his paychecks and bonuses in an offshore account, which his wife had access to. She'd pay the bills on their five thousand square foot house. Make sure they had new cars and the best of the best.

Although he missed being home with his family, he knew he was working for their future. Karl figured he had ten more years of this before he could retire. Walk away and disappear.

Take as much product with him, too. His goal was to sell the house and everything that was not bolted down. His wife had begun to shift money into another offshore account, which they would use to buy an island, if possible.

While their kids were off doing their own things, living their lives, Karl and his wife would be living their ultimate dream: island owners, waking up with a cup of coffee and a bowl, sitting on their deck and watching the sun rise and set.

Karl went back inside. Until this new wrinkle with the monster up the mountain was done, he'd need to worry about the here and now.

He hoped it would get fixed soon enough, especially before the bosses arrived.

CHAPTER TEN

Buck felt a hand on his face and tried to fight it off, fearing they were going to kill him. Mario smiled and put a finger on his lips.

There were four of them surrounding his bunk. Aiden was already awake and getting dressed.

"We're going to find some idiots who aren't in their beds," Mario whispered to Buck. "This could get you out of latrine duty, so hurry up and get dressed."

Buck slipped out of bed, glad he wasn't being beaten. He got dressed, trying to make eye contact with Aiden to see what he thought.

Aiden kept his focus on putting his boots on before following Mario out of the barracks.

"We double up on the three-wheelers," Mario said. He glanced at Buck and Aiden. "Either of you city boys know how to ride?"

"Of course," Aiden said.

"Then you drive and your boyfriend can ride bitch." Mario laughed at his joke as he mounted one of the other trikes. "Stay close but not too close. If you crash into me I'll leave you on top and switch you with the two brothers. Got it?"

Aiden nodded. Buck got on and tried not to grip his friend too much, but he also didn't want to fall off the trike.

They were the second three-wheeler, behind the one Mario was driving, with one more behind them.

"Don't get too close," Buck said over Aiden's shoulder.

"Shut up." Aiden followed along, keeping his distance.

Buck couldn't see much as they started up a trail. He was afraid they were being set up but there was nothing he could do. Aiden was still angry with him, and he'd be a jerk about anything Buck brought up.

In the darkness, with only the feeble light of the trike showcasing a few feet in front of them, Buck was starting to get a headache. He closed his eyes and tried not to panic, either, knowing his fears of the unknown were going to cripple his thoughts.

Buck had to open his eyes soon enough, because they were no longer on a wide trail, bouncing around as they rose up the mountain, slowly circling it.

They stopped in a clearing and Mario waved Aiden to line up next to him. Everyone shut off their trikes.

"From this point we're on foot. One false turn in the dark and you'll fall off the side and likely crash through the barracks and take a couple of idiots out, too," Mario said and laughed.

Aiden walked away from Buck and stood next to Mario, who was handing out pistols to his men. Not Buck or Aiden.

"Hey, don't we get weapons too?" Buck asked.

Aiden frowned and shook his head at Buck.

Mario laughed. "You don't need weapons. You two are going to lead us to the cave."

"Cave?" Buck thought he was going to faint. "Why are we going to the cave?"

Mario sighed and handed Buck and Aiden flashlights. "Because Billy and Clay, the Idiot Brothers, went up there. We think. Hopefully they had the sense to go down the mountain, but we found their tracks and it looks like they went up."

"Why would they go up?" Buck asked. "Isn't there, a, uh…"

"A giant, hairy monster?" Mario laughed. "We tell those stories so no one will go up there. It's an urban legend and nothing more. Now, start walking. There should be a trail. It will take us a long way but it's better than getting lost or falling off the side. Go."

"I hope you're right," Buck said quietly.

Aiden was still staring at Buck. "You lead. I'll be a step behind you."

Buck didn't argue. He started walking, keeping his flashlight beam scanning not only the trail ahead but to either side. He couldn't hear much because Mario and his crew were telling jokes and laughing, stomping through the underbrush loudly.

"These idiots are going to get us killed," Aiden said. "There are mountain lions and bears up here, not to mention the legendary Bigfoot they keep scaring us with."

Buck was surprised his friend was talking to him. Aiden had been so moody the last couple of years. One minute he was joking around with you and the next he was trying to punch you in the face and talk trash about you.

"Hopefully all of their talking will scare off anything that wants to attack us, I guess," Buck said.

"Less chatting, ladies, and make sure you keep on the trail," Mario yelled loudly from only a few feet behind them.

Buck half-turned and shined the light on Mario's chest.

He's scared. I can see it in his eyes, Buck thought.

"Turn around before you get us all killed." Mario was waving his hand with the weapon in it. "Or you'll get yourself killed, if you get my meaning."

"Calm down, bro. It's hard enough to see at night, and with all the noise behind us, we could walk right into a black bear," Aiden said.

Mario laughed. "Maybe a mule deer. We've killed almost all of the big predators over the years. If they're smart they've found another mountain to live on. This is *our* mountain, *bro*."

Buck kept walking, worried the predators behind them were worse than anything they would stumble into. Mario and his men were likely to have them up here so no one would ever find their bodies.

They moved slowly up what they hoped was still the trail until they came to another flat area.

"Stop for a second," Mario said. "Smoke 'em if ya got 'em."

Buck found a large rock to sit down on and Aiden joined him.

Mario's crew pulled out joints and lighters.

"Any for us?" Aiden asked.

Mario shook his head. "And waste some good weed on you two idiots? I don't think so."

Buck was at least happy Aiden had said *any for us* and not *any for me*. That was a good sign.

"I'm sorry I got us into this," Buck said quietly.

Aiden shrugged. "Don't worry about it. Sometimes it happens. You've always been an easy target, Buck. You put yourself into stupid positions and let people walk all over you. Some days I wonder why you even hang out with me. I'm a jerk to you. I use you. I wanted you to come with me this summer not so we could hang out, but so I could get a signing bonus for bringing another worker."

Buck was about to reply, telling Aiden not to overthink it, they were friends, blah blah blah, when someone screamed.

CHAPTER ELEVEN

When there is trouble, one of two things happen: everything is in slow motion, or it is all happening so fast your eyes and brain can't keep up.

It felt like both were happening at once to Buck, and he couldn't fully process what any of it meant.

One of Mario's crew screamed and at first Mario laughed, if only for a couple of seconds.

Buck thought he saw a giant, hairy arm, five times as thick as his own, swinging from the darkness and snatching one of the men away from the flashlight beams.

Everyone crowded together on the trail, lights moving everywhere so much Buck thought he'd get a strobe light headache.

If he survived the next few minutes.

"What just happened?" Mario said quietly, as if he were asking someone to pass the salt at the dinner table.

Buck could see the fear in Mario's eyes. In everyone's eyes.

"It was Bigfoot," one of the crew said. "That thing is real."

Mario was shaking his head. "No. No way. Someone is messing with us. Nice try." He got on his trike. "We need to continue."

"No way," one of the men said. "I'm going back to the cabin, where it's safe."

Mario was off the trike and had a pistol jammed under the man's chin. "You are going to follow orders. That's exactly what's going to happen. Understand? If you go back down to camp, Gestapo Karl is going to kill you... if I don't kill you first."

Buck could see the man was weighing all of his options, and none of them looked good.

Mario pushed the man away but kept his weapon in hand. "You can ride alone and lead us. The sooner we find those two runaways the quicker we can go back."

Buck and Aiden got back on their trike and waited for the man to start moving, which he did.

Mario and the other crew member were behind them now, and Buck didn't like Mario at his back.

Aiden followed but kept a good distance, which was a good move to Buck. If that thing attacked the first trike they might be able to turn and outrun it.

Buck felt trapped. If they went back down the mountain, Mario was right: Gestapo Karl was going to kill them for not finding the two brothers. If they continued up, the Bigfoot might get them.

He'd seen the hairy arm and knew it wasn't someone messing around. It wasn't a joke or a prop, either. It was an actual arm of a monster, ending in black claws and sharp tips.

The man snatched had let out one scream before disappearing, which meant he was already dead.

Bigfoot killed him immediately. Shut him up, Buck thought.

The thought of such a large creature, able to sneak up on an armed group, and simply drag one away in seconds, was frightening.

The three-wheelers kept heading up the mountain and into what Buck thought was certain death. Maybe they could get to wherever the brothers were and rescue them before the Bigfoot rushed to them, too.

Maybe Bigfoot is busy eating the snatched man, Buck thought.

He kept looking around, worried the last thing he'd see was the massive arm, a second before it yanked him off the back of the three-wheeler and into the dark woods.

Around each turn, Buck could feel Aiden tense, and he didn't blame his friend. The monster could be simply standing on the trail, waiting for them.

Buck didn't like when the lone man ahead of them disappeared around a turn, even if for a few seconds.

He wouldn't be surprised to see a wrecked trike, covered in blood, around the next bend in the trail.

We're making too much noise, Buck thought. The three trikes were loud. He was sure the noise was echoing all over the mountain.

Buck wanted to go home. He wondered how he could extract himself from all of this, once they got back to the camp and safety.

As if anywhere on this mountain was safe.

He wondered how Mario was going to spin this to Gestapo Karl. A giant monster had taken one of the men and he was likely already dead, ripped apart.

We're all gonna die, Buck thought.

"Loosen up, bro. You're holding me too tightly. I'm not your girlfriend," Aiden yelled over his shoulder.

"Sorry," Buck mumbled and tried to relax but it was impossible. He was fighting back tears. He knew he was shaking, but the vibration of the trike was hiding it. He was sure Aiden was shaking in fear, too. He wasn't that tough.

Up and up they went, and Buck wanted to shut his eyes but knew he'd need to see where they were going and when he needed to shift to the left or right to help Aiden and to keep from falling over and off the three-wheeler.

Off the mountain to certain death. Or up the mountain… to certain death.

Ahead, in a straightaway, the single rider stopped and pulled off to the side in a small clearing. He jumped off and shined his flashlight ahead.

Aiden pulled up behind him and Mario a second later.

"What's the holdup?" Mario asked.

"I thought I saw something, in the treeline, pacing with me," the man said.

Mario laughed. "No way that thing can keep up."

"Well, it is and it did. Do you want to go in front and prove me wrong?" The man was glaring at Mario.

"No. I want you to get us to the cave so we can see if the brothers are in there, dead or alive," Mario said. "Then we head back down and we'll all have a fun story to tell for years to come."

"About someone getting eaten by a Bigfoot?" Aiden asked.

Mario sighed. "There is no Bigfoot. Just a mountain lion or a bear. That's all. We're wasting time. Keep moving."

Everyone mounted up again and the trikes began to move along the trail.

Buck could see the fear in Aiden's eyes and knew his own was being reflected back.

How much longer? I'm going to wet myself, Buck thought.

They drove for what felt like hours but might only have been less than one, when the lead man stopped and pulled over again. He dismounted and shined his flashlight ahead.

"We're here. At the cave entrance," Mario said, coming up from behind and slapping Buck on the back like they were old friends. "Now we need to fan out and find these two idiot brothers."

CHAPTER TWELVE

Buck and Aiden stayed together, slowly moving in the opposite direction of Mario and his remaining men. They searched the ground for any signs.

Giant footprints, human boot prints, blood, guts, gore.

All they saw was the deep, thick underbrush and endless trees, all looking menacing in the darkness the second their beams hit them.

No one went near the cave entrance.

Their flashlight beams didn't penetrate more than a few feet, and most of the light was blocked by trees and thick foliage.

"This is ridiculous. They're either miles away and safe or they're dead," Aiden said quietly.

"I don't want to stumble upon a dead body." Buck heard a twig snap and turned quickly, but it was Mario and one of his men coming up.

"We check the cave itself and then go back to camp, I guess," Mario said.

"Then let's get this over with." Buck already knew he'd be volunteered for cave duty. "If you want me to go into the cave, I'll need a weapon."

"No chance," Mario said.

"Then no chance either of us go inside." Aiden shined his light in Mario's eyes. "Where's the other guy?"

Everyone looked around. Mario called out for the missing man, who'd been the one to lead them the last part of the journey.

They all listened but the man didn't answer, and they didn't hear him moving through the underbrush.

"When you two go into the cave, see if you can find him, too. Maybe that's where he went to search," Mario said.

Everyone still alive knew that wasn't true. Another man had been taken by the Bigfoot.

Aiden held out his hand. "A weapon, please."

Buck held out his hand, too.

"Be quick. In and out. If you see anything out of the ordinary, call out," Mario said. He handed each of them a pistol.

Buck chuckled. "Be quick? Do you really think we're going to take our sweet time in there?"

Mario was in Buck's face. "No lip from you, boy. Got it? In and out. Hurry up." Mario had his own weapon out, and waved it at Buck. "I'll be right here, waiting for your report."

Aiden didn't move, looking at Buck, who sighed.

"I'll lead," Buck said and all four men walked to the mouth of the cave.

Even with their two flashlights, they couldn't see much of the inside of the cave. It was wide but within ten feet turned to the right.

The ground was well-worn. Not much dirt. A lot of rock, and Buck noticed claw marks on the walls.

This is not a good idea, Buck thought.

He took a few steps, trying to will his body to keep moving forward. His fight or flight was kicking in, and he knew which one would win if it wasn't for an armed Mario blocking his way.

Aiden was able to stand next to Buck, which made Buck feel slightly safer.

They turned with the cave and saw it split up ahead.

"Two tunnels," Aiden turned and said over his shoulder.

"Split up and figure out what's in each. Hurry up," Mario said.

Both Buck and Aiden shook their heads. No way they were going to split up and either get lost or get eaten.

"Which way?" Buck asked.

"To the left. Whenever we get to a fork, we always take the left. I read or heard that somewhere. So we don't get lost." Aiden started to walk to the left and Buck followed.

The ground was uneven but there were no huge gaps or holes. The walls were wet and Buck pointed his flashlight to the high ceiling and could see water dripping between cracks. As they moved deeper into the tunnel he realized there was more and more mountain rising above them.

They took another left turn at yet another fork, and both stopped.

At the end of the tunnel they could see a large pool of water.

Buck could smell a musty odor, like a wet dog.

They approached cautiously, but the pool of water was shallow, collected from all the water coming from above.

"Look," Aiden said.

Buck followed his beam and gasped.

On the far end of the pool a set of rocks rose from the water, and on it was piled perhaps hundreds of bones. All picked clean. Nothing but the white of skulls and femurs and all the rest.

Buck didn't see any human skulls, mostly deer and grizzly and mountain lion, if he had to guess, based on the shapes and sizes.

Most of the bones had been snapped in half and scattered on the rock. Some of them had been thrown or fallen into the pool, too.

"Time to find another way," Aiden said.

They turned and headed back until they found the cross tunnel again, going to the right this time. Buck tried to remember where they were and when they'd changed direction, but he was panicking inside. Something had killed all of those animals, and he'd seen the massive arm that could do it.

This tunnel dead-ended in a hundred feet, with a crack in the wall. Aiden pressed against it, trying to see if there was anything inside.

"Anything?" Buck asked, watching the way they'd come in. If the Bigfoot was in the caves they'd be trapped.

"Not that I can see, but we might be able to squeeze inside," Aiden said.

"And why would we have to do that?" Buck asked.

"In the event we're trapped in the caves. Duh." Aiden walked past Buck. "Time to get out of here. There's nobody around. No one alive, anyway."

"There is still another tunnel we haven't explored," Buck said.

Aiden shook his head. "We've been here for too long. Mario might have already left us behind."

Buck didn't see a need to argue. He was creeped out being in the cave system, and didn't want to run into Bigfoot.

If we survive this ordeal, this will be some story to tell back home, Buck thought.

Aiden shook his head and sighed. "How do we get into these messes?"

Buck followed Aiden to the next fork in the tunnel, but it looked different. "Uh… are we lost?"

CHAPTER THIRTEEN

It seemed impossible they were in an unknown part of the cave system, one they hadn't yet traversed, but inside the mountain things got weird quickly.

All that rock all around you, the pressure of it, the claustrophobia mixed in with the fear of being ripped apart, limb by limb, from a Bigfoot... it was all too much.

"Should we turn back?" Buck asked.

Aiden looked behind them, using his flashlight. Then he turned and looked the way they were going. "I have no idea."

"That's not very helpful," Buck said.

"No, it most certainly is not. This way." Aiden kept moving forward. "Turn off your flashlight. The batteries might run out."

"I'm hoping to leave before that happens," Buck said.

"So am I. Just do it."

Buck turned off his flashlight and felt naked. Afraid. He kept glancing behind but without light it was a dark mass following them and nothing more.

A foot behind me could be a monster, waiting for the perfect moment to slice my head off, Buck thought.

"We need to find the exit," Buck said.

Aiden stopped. "Wait... did you hear that?"

Buck heard nothing but kept his mouth shut. He was shaking and glad he wasn't trying to use the flashlight, because he thought he wouldn't be able to keep the beam straight enough to see.

They stood motionless for nearly a minute, Aiden shining the light in front and behind them, but there was only rock and dirt.

"Maybe water dripping somewhere," Aiden said quietly.

Buck doubted whatever he'd heard was anything but a Bigfoot stalking its prey.

They were its prey.

They started to move again slowly, coming to another fork in the tunnel. It looked like all of the other ones.

"Shouldn't we be going left?" Buck asked.

Aiden shrugged. "We might be turned around, which means we need to go right now."

Buck had no idea if that was smart but didn't question Aiden. One way or another they'd need to find the exit.

With nothing else to do, they went to the right and followed the tunnel.

Maybe a hundred feet ahead they saw it branched into three different tunnels. One went straight ahead, while the one to the left looked like it descended slowly deeper and the one on the right rose up.

"Obviously, we go up," Aiden said.

"We've definitely never been here."

Aiden chuckled. "Considering this is the first time we've ever been in these caves… yeah. Duh, bro."

"You don't have to be a jerk. You know what I mean," Buck said. "Lead the way, *bro*."

Aiden looked angry but he turned and shone his light into the right tunnel.

To Buck it looked like all of the others.

Aiden started walking and Buck was a step behind.

The tunnel was definitely rising slowly with each step. Buck wondered how deep into the caves they were and if this led back to where they'd entered, or another exit.

Or a dead end. Or the lair of the Bigfoot, where he ate animals and humans.

Buck stopped when he heard a noise behind him, an echo from far away. He stopped Aiden and they both listened but nothing was heard after a few seconds.

Aiden pointed the way they were going and nodded. Buck nodded back. It might be a good thing to not talk, use body language so nothing could sneak up on them.

Buck remembered the quickness of the hairy arm, coming out of nowhere, and snatching that guy.

He shuddered and tried not to panic. He wanted to scream, to run as fast as he could until he found the exit.

Aiden looked like he was keeping his cool, but Buck knew he was just as scared and on the edge of panic. They'd known each other a long time, and Buck knew Aiden would always play it cool until afterwards, when he'd admit how scared he was.

Buck glanced back and turned on his flashlight for a second, but there was nothing but rock behind them.

They kept walking until Aiden stopped short and moved to the side.

In front of them were two things: a crack up ahead in the rocks, where sunlight seeped through.

Buck smiled. They were going to be fine. It was already morning, which meant by now a search party would be organized and someone would be looking for them.

Gestapo Karl knew where they were, right? If Mario had returned last night, he would tell them that Buck and Aiden had gone into the caves… right?

Buck shook his head, because he knew Mario wasn't going to tell anyone what had happened. He'd blame Buck and Aiden for going into the caves. He'd say he tried to warn them not to go, that it was dangerous.

Mario was going to throw them under the bus and tell everyone they were likely dead.

Aiden was shining his light on the ground.

Buck took a step forward and looked to see, too.

The tunnel floor a couple of feet ahead of them was gone.

A deep, dark abyss. At least ten feet across, with no way to go forward.

Buck found a small rock on the ground and tossed it into the pit.

They never heard it hit the bottom, if there was even a bottom.

The sunlight may as well be a thousand miles away.

"We're still trapped. Time to head back the way we came," Aiden said.

Buck could only follow along.

CHAPTER FOURTEEN

Aiden was getting tired. He was keeping it together because he knew Buck was one bad thing away from losing his mind and freaking out. Likely falling to the ground, crying, in the fetal position.

His best friend could be such a baby sometimes.

I need to get us out of here, Aiden thought. His thoughts were clear for the first time in years. He'd gone through life getting high every chance he got, and that was a lot.

To Aiden there was no better feeling in the world than getting high. He couldn't understand how he'd survived without smoking. His home life was a mess, school was a joke, and he really only had Buck as his friend. Loyal Buck.

The kids he sold pot to weren't his friends. He realized that now. They were faking it to get a discount or to smoke a free joint with Aiden. None of them cared about him.

Only Buck, shivering at his side, scared out of his mind right now.

I gotta be strong and save us, Aiden thought.

But he had no idea where they were in the cave system. They'd somehow missed a wrong turn, even though he only remembered a couple of side tunnels initially. Maybe one or two had also cut back and they hadn't paid attention or seen them as they walked.

What seemed like an hour later they stepped back into the room with the water and bones.

"Okay, this is good," Aiden said.

Buck looked like he'd been crying. Aiden made sure not to shine the light on his friend's face and embarrass him.

"How is this good?" Buck turned away, wiping his eyes. "We're in an endless loop. We'll join the dead here soon enough. I bet Bigfoot didn't even eat them, they were lost in the cave and came here to die like the rest."

Aiden wanted to point out the claw and bite marks on the bones but thought it would be a bad idea. Buck was already freaked out and it wouldn't be a long step for him to be too far gone.

"I think I can get us out of here. I know where we took a wrong turn, so it shouldn't be hard to backtrack the right way," Aiden said. He smiled at Buck.

Buck sighed. "Then lead the way. I want to go home."

Aiden was also done with this job and camp and Mario and all of it. He wanted to get down the mountain but drive the trike straight to his van and be done.

Maybe McDonalds is hiring, Aiden thought. He'd lose the pay he'd made in the few days they'd been here, and the gas it cost to drive over, but he was done. He'd lie to his father about them being sent home because there were too many workers this year. Find something else to do, closer to home.

Aiden patted Buck on his shoulder. "We're going to get out. Trust me. We're the heroes in this videogame."

"This isn't a videogame," Buck said quietly.

"Life is a videogame." Aiden started to lead the way back, hoping he'd actually remember where he went the wrong way.

They walked and Aiden was feeling confident he knew where he was going.

His flashlight started to dim.

"Hey, uh, your light," Buck said, as if Aiden hadn't noticed it. "Here, take mine."

They switched flashlights. Aiden wondered how long before they both went dead.

Trapped in the caves without light was an awful thought and Aiden tried to clear it from his mind but he couldn't. He thought of good things: smoking weed, seeing women naked, tacos and the time he dropped acid.

None of it could clear the fear from his mind, though.

Aiden picked up the pace. They were back at a fork in the tunnel. Aiden couldn't remember which way they'd gone last time.

"I think we went right because you said it was reversed," Buck said.

Aiden started down the left hand path. Within thirty feet they came to another split in the tunnels. There was something shiny on the ground and he bent down.

He dusted it off with his hand and smiled. "Look, bro. It's a railroad track."

Buck helped Aiden wipe off more of the track. "No, not the railroad. This was a mine."

They found the other side of the tracks, and knew it was too small for anything bigger than a minecart. In either direction they could see the faint outline of it, buried in dust and dirt.

"We found a way out," Aiden said.

He shone the light in both directions.

"Yeah, but which way is which? I don't think either tunnel slopes up," Buck said.

"Then we go left. Isn't that the rule?" Aiden asked.

If Buck had an argument, he kept it to himself and followed Aiden.

"Tracks mean an exit somewhere. Right? We just need to check and make sure at crossroads we don't lose them," Aiden said.

He had renewed hope they'd escape. He moved quicker now, almost in a jog.

All we need to do is get out before the light goes out, Aiden thought.

He knew it was easier said than done.

They came to the end of this tunnel, but it spilled out to the left and to the right. The tracks went both ways, a lazy curve.

In the center of the T there was an old minecart, busted into pieces, only two sides of it still intact along with the cracked bottom. The wheels were bent, one of them missing.

Aiden shone the light inside, hoping it was filled with gold nuggets. Getting rich might be a nice plus side for this adventure.

There was nothing but dirt.

"Hey, aren't old mines supposed to be filled with rats?" Buck asked.

Aiden nodded.

"Then where are they?" Buck was shaking again.

Aiden knew where they were: all eaten by Bigfoot. There weren't even spiders in the tunnels. Did the monster live off anything he could get his huge hands on? It seemed likely, considering all of the bones.

Did Bigfoot hibernate in the winter? How far from the cave would it go to collect a meal? Why were there still animals on the mountain, if they knew a predator was inside it?

So many questions were spinning through Aiden's head right now.

None of the answers he came up with led to a happy ending, a positive way for them to leave the mountain.

"Let's keep going," Aiden said, shining his light down the left tunnel.

CHAPTER FIFTEEN

The tunnel began to slope down and at first Buck wanted to ask Aiden why they weren't turning around and going the other way, but then it began sloping upwards.

Another minecart, this one still on the tracks, blocked their way. To either side the walls had begun to collapse, so there was no way around it.

"I guess we go up and over," Aiden said.

Buck nodded. "It also might mean Bigfoot never came this way, because he would've destroyed the minecart."

"True." Aiden smiled. "I'll go first."

Buck watched Aiden climb awkwardly over the minecart. Dirt fell from the ceiling but Buck didn't want to turn on the weak flashlight and see. He was afraid of what was up there, too. Maybe a lot of loose rocks and dirt, which would bury them alive.

Calm down and get a grip, Buck thought.

He did some deep breaths and tried to control his thoughts. He knew they would survive. No one was getting eaten, no one was getting buried.

Buck held his breath when he couldn't see the light and everything went black. He moved his hand out in front of his face but couldn't see it. He was completely blind.

"Come on. Use the flashlight," Aiden said from the darkness, spooking Buck.

Buck didn't need to be told twice. He turned it on but the light was so dim it was hard to see with it. He climbed up onto the minecart like Aiden had done and slowly moved across it to the other side.

Aiden had his light shining on the ground so Buck missed stepping on a bunch of rocks and got down safely.

They kept walking, following the rails.

Now they saw cobwebs and heard the scurrying of rats.

"We're safer in this part of the mine," Aiden said.

"Unless we get bitten by a venomous snake or a mountain lion has a lair," Buck reminded his friend. "We're safe when we get into sunlight."

"True." Aiden was walking faster now and Buck stumbled to keep up.

They were slowly rising, swiping their hands because the cobwebs were thicker.

Buck smacked a few small spiders off him, afraid they were going to sink their fangs into his neck and poison him. He had no idea which spiders were dangerous, so he treated them all like monsters and killed them whenever they appeared.

Ahead was a wooden structure, rotting just off the path. The rails went right past it but a set went through the structure, too.

Aiden stopped and shined the light. "Wow. That can't be real."

Buck looked and gasped.

A giant gold boulder was on the ground, having crushed through a wooden table years ago. It was the size of a basketball, maybe bigger.

"That's worth millions, right?" Aiden asked.

Buck had to agree. They approached it slowly, the wooden floor of the structure creaking as they moved.

Both of them touched it and smiled.

"Does it feel like gold? Does it feel real?" Aiden asked.

"How should I know? I've never had a gold rock this big before." Buck chuckled. They were rich.

"We need to take it with us," Aiden said.

"How? No way we can carry it."

Aiden tried to push it over. "Then we roll it out with us."

The gold ball didn't move.

"Why did they leave it here? That makes no sense. If it was too heavy, maybe chop it into smaller pieces and carry it out," Buck said.

Aiden shined the flashlight past the structure. There were claw marks all over the walls. He took a few steps and saw more of them.

"I guess Bigfoot came up this way at some point," Buck said.

"We can't leave it here," Aiden groaned. "We need to figure out where we are and come back for it, I guess."

"We can do like Hansel and Gretel," Buck said.

"Do you have breadcrumbs with you?"

Buck smiled. "No, but maybe we use a rock to scrape the walls as we get to another split in the tunnels."

"Great idea," Aiden said. "We obviously tell no one about this."

"Obviously."

Aiden and Buck both found a sizable rock. Not that they would do much against Bigfoot, but they could help them to relocate the gold later.

If there was a later, Buck thought.

Aiden scraped a rough A on the wall to the left. "Always to the left, that way we know on the way back it will be on the right. Got it?"

Buck nodded.

There was another fork in the tunnel, but only one had the mine rails, so they went that way and marked the wall.

Buck knew they'd been gone many hours. Had Mario made it back? Had he told Gestapo Karl they were dead or had run off? No way they'd send a search party and risk more deaths.

He wondered if Gestapo Karl would shut everything down now, or if this was just the cost of doing business.

"Our parents are going to freak out if we don't come home," Aiden said.

"We have all summer, though, is the problem. If we die today it will be weeks before anyone back home would realize we'd been killed." Buck kept glancing back over his shoulder but it was too dark to see anything sneaking up on them.

"By then, Gestapo Karl will have had plenty of time to spin a story about us running away or something," Aiden said.

They kept moving, following the rails left a long time ago by miners. Obviously, these mountains had plenty of gold in them back in the day.

Still has a lot of gold, Buck thought, thinking of the large chunk they'd had to leave behind.

They rounded a bend in the tunnel and Aiden stopped short.

Buck could see it now, too: light at the end of the tunnel. Sunlight ahead. The exit to the caves.

Aiden ran ahead and Buck was about to call out for him to slow down when a shadow passed over the ground right past the exit.

A very large shadow.

Buck fell against the tunnel wall, trying to make himself look small.

Aiden had dropped down onto one knee.

The stench of the monster wafted into the tunnel and Buck nearly puked.

CHAPTER SIXTEEN

Mario was alone. One minute he was talking to his second, Smitty, and then… Smitty was gone, only the rustling of branches letting Mario know in which direction he'd gone.

He's dead. The Bigfoot got him, Mario thought.

It was now early morning, the sun rising slowly up the mountain and bathing it all in orange light.

Until tonight he believed there was no monster up on the mountain other than the usual mountain lion or a bear. Maybe other marijuana growers from the other side of the mountain wanting to scare them off.

Now… Mario knew. He'd seen it, if only briefly.

Mario had taken a step toward where Smitty had gone and there it was.

A Bigfoot, maybe seven or eight feet tall, dark hair covering the body, the face like pure evil, claws and fangs. It glanced at Mario for a second before turning and bounding off into the thick woods.

Mario also knew what that glance meant: you aren't going to escape. I'll be back. Let me just drop off this meal in my cave and then I will hunt you down like prey.

Those two idiots who'd gone into the cave were certainly dead.

Mario hadn't seen the other guy he'd brought with him, either, and assumed he was killed.

I'm the only one alive, the only one who can tell Gestapo Karl and the camp what was really up here, Mario thought.

Even when Gestapo Karl talked about the Bigfoot like it was real and they sacrificed animals to it each season so it would leave them alone, Mario thought it all a big joke. Like it was a ritual they needed to do in order to keep traditions alive.

Something to scare the workers into doing their job and not wandering off to get caught by the Feds. Mario didn't know if anyone had ever been recruited by the government to try and take them down. He doubted it, considering they were still operational.

He'd heard of other camps being raided in the past, and he'd been working at one the summer before he started here, but he was on a supply run when they heard the Feds had swarmed it.

Mario never wanted to do anything else, though. The next year, through some friends of friends, he'd hooked up with this group. Made great money and got in good with the camp boss, so he never had to do any of the awful and menial jobs.

Why are you even thinking about any of this? Time to run, Mario thought.

He ran to the trikes and started one up, looking around for an attack. He knew the monster was fast because until he'd stopped to look at Mario, he'd never been in the same spot long enough to be truly seen.

Mario wished he could wipe the image from his mind but knew as long as he lived it would be there.

He hoped he lived to be very old, sitting and spitting up in a nursing home, telling the nurses and doctors about his encounter with Bigfoot. They'd never believe him, but Mario would know.

As soon as he started moving, he realized there was no straight shot down the mountain. Lots of precarious turns and spots you could fall over the side if you were going too fast or not being careful.

Don't panic. You got this, Mario thought.

He started down the path, hoping he could still follow the way they'd come up the mountain. There were so many secondary trails and spots where there was no trail.

Mario had to relax if he was going to live, and not only worry about a Bigfoot attack. He was speeding up and taking turns too sharply, going up on two wheels and bouncing too much.

He needed to keep control.

Slowly down around the next turn, he glanced to his left and saw the massive drop over the side. There was no chance he'd survive a fall.

On better days Mario might like the view. He'd sit on a rock and admire the world below him, smoking a joint and smiling.

Now it looked like a drop to his certain death.

Coming around another bend too fast, Mario ducked when he saw a moss-covered tree branch level with his head.

Mario screamed when the branch moved, and he knew he'd been inches from being decapitated by the Bigfoot's arm.

He looked back over his shoulder but didn't see the creature.

Is he toying with me? No way he could've missed me. All he had to do was lower his arm, Mario thought.

He hoped Bigfoot had taken his shot and wouldn't follow him down the mountain. Maybe it was only to scare him to stay away from his cave and his property.

Mario took a turn too fast and the trike shot into the underbrush off to the side. He overcorrected and the trike spun out of control.

He screamed as the trike lifted into the air, threatening to buck him like he was on a bronco.

Mario remembered, as a kid, visiting his uncle's ranch in Texas and getting to ride an old pony. He still remembered the thrill of it as the horse trotted around in a circle, Mario imagining he was a cowboy.

This was nothing like that, fast and furious and deadly.

Mario saw the tree ahead as the trike started to go in one direction, which was getting too close to the edge of the mountain.

He tried to leap off the trike but was paralyzed with fear.

Ahead was certain death, too: he'd either follow the trike off the side or into a very large tree, overhanging the gorge.

Mario closed his eyes and tried to scramble off the trike, managing to get off it but not away from it as it went over the side.

He slammed face-first into the tree but was not knocked out.

Opening his eyes, Mario wished he hadn't.

He was lying on top of a horizontal part of the tree, his face looking down into the abyss. His body hurt and he didn't know if he could move, and afraid if he did he'd slip over the side.

Mario slowly turned his head to see he was at least ten feet onto the tree from the side of the mountain, and at least five feet below the ridge.

I need to shimmy back to the mountain and then reach up, pull myself up, and crawl to freedom, Mario thought.

He didn't think he was on the right side of the mountain, either, so shouting for help wouldn't work.

It would also give away his position if the monster was nearby.

Maybe when it was done eating Smitty and all the rest it would come for Mario, looking for a snack.

Mario began to cry as the tree shook, buffeted by the rising wind.

CHAPTER SEVENTEEN

Buck stayed where he was and Aiden slowly moved back to join him.

The shadow was swaying back and forth, as if waiting to ambush them if they left the relative safety of the cave.

Aiden leaned in close to Buck, his mouth near his ear. "I think I hear a motor. Do you?"

Buck nodded. He knew what it meant: they were left here to die. Mario and his crew had taken off, back down the mountain.

The Bigfoot must've heard it as well, because they heard a thud outside, followed by a tree crashing to the ground in their sight, snapped in half like it was a toothpick.

"Bigfoot is following them," Buck said and faintly smiled. It meant in order to escape, they'd need to walk down the mountain.

Unless a trike was left behind.

They took their time exiting the cave, afraid it was a trick and Bigfoot was standing above them, ready to pounce.

Buck turned, wincing, but all he saw was rock, treetops and the blue sky above them.

"Are we okay? Do you think we can survive down the mountain?" Aiden asked.

Buck shook his head. He was realistic enough to know they were far from being safe. "First, let's figure out where we are and if we can find the trikes again."

"That might be wasting time, when we can start running down the mountain," Aiden said.

"And risk a slow going and the Bigfoot hearing us. He'll be more than aware of the trails we need to take," Buck said. "If we hurry, we can find a trike and rush down before he has a chance to get us." Buck knew it was a risk. All of it was at this point, though.

Ideally, if they could find a three-wheeler they'd have a better chance of outrunning Bigfoot. If they were forced to walk they'd be easy prey for it.

Damned if you do, damned if you don't, Buck thought.

"If the trikes are all gone, we've wasted a lot of time looking for them," Aiden said. "Too risky. I say we head down to the camp."

Buck was annoyed at his friend, who he usually always followed blindly.

"No. I'm going to find a trike. We might be really close to them, just around the next bend." Buck started to walk to his left, figuring it was as good as any direction to go.

He tried to find a path to use but there were only trees and tight underbrush to fight through.

Aiden was right behind him now. "Fine. We'll do it your way. If Bigfoot rips me apart I'll be happy to say I told you so."

"Then let's really hope you're wrong," Buck said. "Look. I see the trail."

They'd only gone about twenty feet when Buck spied a strip of dirt and tire tracks on it.

Buck fought through and managed to get his feet on the trail.

"Is it this way or that way, though?" Aiden asked.

To the left it seemed to rise slowly. It all looked different in the morning light. They'd not been able to see much on the night ride up the mountain.

"Definitely this way," Buck said, trying to sound like he knew what he was talking about.

He had no real clue and this was a fifty-fifty guess for him.

Buck hoped it wasn't the wrong one, although even if they were headed in the wrong direction, it meant they were going down the mountain.

They followed the trail, trying not to make too much noise.

It was a beautiful day. Not many clouds in the sky. Birds chirping in the trees. Not too hot. A nice breeze blowing, sometimes a gust that brought cool air.

I hope we're close to where we started from, Buck thought.

They'd traveled a long way in the tunnels. He hoped it wasn't miles away from their starting point, far from the three-wheelers. At some of the tunnel splits they'd doubled back, once or twice, so maybe they were closer than he thought.

Buck stopped every now and then to listen for Bigfoot.

They'd been walking for far too long. By now Bigfoot had either chased down the trikes and was on his way back to his cave with the bodies, or he had given up and waited in ambush by the trikes left.

If there were any three-wheelers left.

Aiden stumbled behind him but didn't fall down. He wasn't complaining but Buck had known him long enough to feel the heat of his anger.

This was a mistake. We should've started to head down, Buck thought.

Buck stopped when he heard something big crashing down the mountain above and ahead of them.

He spread his feet as the ground shook, noting Aiden had done the same.

"There," Aiden said and pointed.

It wasn't Bigfoot, but a large boulder rushing down the mountain, knocking down small trees and ripping a path through the woods. They could only watch as it disappeared across the trail.

Buck looked up to see if there were anymore coming down, but he couldn't see any.

Was it Bigfoot trying to crush us, or give a warning? It could simply be a natural occurrence, Buck thought.

He hoped it was a rock falling down after all this time. He'd seen quite a few of them while they were ascending the mountain last night.

"Let's keep moving," Aiden said.

They both kept walking, heads swiveling so nothing snuck up on them.

As if they'd have time to see or even fight off Bigfoot if it was around the next bend.

Buck took a few deep breaths as he walked and tried to remain calm. They'd been through quite an ordeal the last few hours, without sleep or food. Not even a drop of water. And yet, he felt good. He had a purpose, which was simple enough.

Stay alive.

Aiden looked miserable to Buck, and he was close to his breaking point. A lot closer than Buck, which almost made him smile.

For once, I'm in charge. I'm the one who is calling the shots, Buck thought.

When they'd been in trouble in the past, like the time they had to run from the cops because Aiden had tried to sell weed to an undercover narc, Buck had only been there as the tagalong. He wasn't making any money, only there as a friend.

Aiden had led the way, the route to escape, and Buck had followed blindly.

Like he always did.

Over fences, under cars and across lawns and parks, Buck had kept Aiden in his sights as they ran.

Eventually, they'd managed to slip into the back of a pizza place and drop down into a booth, taking off their jackets and wiping the sweat from their faces with napkins.

It had been harrowing, and Buck had nearly crapped himself a couple of times, but they laughed at the near miss. Then they ordered a pizza and bragged about it for weeks.

There wasn't going to be much bragging about their time on the mountain so far.

Lots of death. Lots of near misses so far.

Buck hoped their luck didn't run out.

"There," Aiden nearly shouted and pointed over Buck's shoulder.

Their luck hadn't run out.

Two of the three-wheelers were parked where they'd left them last night in the dark.

CHAPTER EIGHTEEN

"We take both," Buck said to Aiden, who immediately sat down on one of the trikes and motioned for Buck to sit behind him. "That way, if need be, we can split up and Bigfoot can't get both of us."

"Good idea," Aiden said. By the look on his face, he understood Buck's words. They had a better chance of one of them surviving on two trikes than both on one.

Buck got on a trike and started it up, leading the way back the way they'd come. Aiden was close behind but not too close, which was good.

If Bigfoot attacked or another boulder came down the mountain, or any of a dozen other deadly things happened, they needed to be far enough away from one another. At least one of them had to live to tell their story.

And eventually come back and get the gold basketball.

Buck took off, knowing the sound of the trikes was going to draw the monster. He hoped he was so far down the mountain or already inside his cave.

Heading down in the light was much easier than going up in the dark, but Buck didn't want to get too cocky and speed. He took each turn slower than usual and made sure he had plenty of notice if something was in the way.

Aiden was still keeping up and pacing back a bit.

Buck rounded another corner and saw three-wheeler tracks ripping through the dirt and veering off toward the side of the mountain. He glanced back at Aiden, who waved his hand to keep going.

What if Mario and whoever else was alive was hurt? Since he'd only taken one trike, there could only be two left at the most. It might not even be Mario, one or two of his lackeys.

Buck knew they should keep heading down the mountain.

He knew he needed to worry about himself and Aiden only.

If the roles were reversed, Mario's crew wouldn't think twice about leaving them behind.

Buck turned off his trike and ignored Aiden, who threw his hands up and turned off his.

"We need to go," Aiden said.

"One second. I can't leave someone if they need help. Neither can you." Buck started to follow the trike tracks.

"I can. I really can leave these jerks," Aiden said.

Buck stopped and looked at Aiden. "Then go. Leave me to do the right thing and you worry only about yourself. Hopefully Bigfoot doesn't rip me to pieces. Although… I'm sure you could live with that. Right?"

Aiden gave him the finger. "Let's hurry this up and get out of here."

Buck didn't hear moaning or calls for help, but more importantly he didn't hear Bigfoot crashing through, knocking over trees.

The dirt stopped and there was twenty feet of solid rock between Buck and the drop-off, but he assumed the trike hadn't turned or veered off.

He went to the edge. Aiden hooked a finger through Buck's belt loop to keep him from falling over, especially since the wind was strong.

Buck couldn't see the trike below, but there were a lot of small trees and overgrowth on the side of the mountain.

"See anything? We need to get going," Aiden said.

"Nothing… wait." Buck knelt down and saw Mario, clinging to a tree. He traced it back to the side of the cliff and saw where the tree began, which was a few feet below them.

"Mario? Can you hear me? Are you alright?" Buck asked, kneeling down next to the start of the tree. "Can you climb up?" Buck held a hand out, Aiden still holding onto him.

Buck didn't want to climb out onto the tree to rescue Mario, fearing it might be too much weight. The tree was swaying in the wind.

Mario was wrapped around the thick tree and looked like he'd been crying, his face wet and dirty.

"Come on. Take my hand," Buck said.

"He's in shock. Leave him. We'll go and get help," Aiden said.

Buck shook his head. "No way. We can't leave him like this. At some point the wind will knock him off or the tree will break, or Bigfoot will find him."

Mario wasn't moving. He had a tight grip on the tree with both his arms and his legs.

Buck tried to move out further but Aiden pulled him back.

"No way. You're not going out there. We'll come back for him. All three of us can't ride back, anyway," Aiden said.

"I can't just leave him." Buck was torn. This might be Mario's only chance of getting down alive. If he could even be coaxed off the tree.

Aiden was looking around. "Did you hear that?"

Buck stood up. "Hear what?"

There was nothing to hear. Not even the birds, who'd gone silent. Only the breeze rustling the leaves on the trees now.

"Time to go," Aiden said. "Before it finds us."

"Don't leave me," Mario shouted, breaking the silence. "I don't want to fall and die."

"Then get up and take my hand," Buck said, going back down on his knees. "Hurry up. Come with us if you want to live."

"I want to live," Mario said and began slowly moving on the tree, an inch at a time.

"Hurry," Buck said. At this rate it would take Mario an hour to get close enough for Buck to attempt to pull him up to safety.

"It is coming. I can hear it," Aiden said close to Buck. "We need to go."

"Not without Mario." Buck was leaning as far as he thought he could without losing his balance or not being able to help Mario up. "Just a few more minutes."

"We don't even have seconds," Aiden said, his voice cracking.

Buck was staring at Mario. "I need you to move faster. I need you to hurry."

Mario seemed to pick up the pace but he was still going too slow, and kept looking down and stopping.

"I see it coming down the mountain," Aiden said and yanked Buck back, knocking him on his butt. "We're out of time."

Mario had been shimmying across the tree, but as Aiden's words seemed to sink in, he got up on his hands and knees and started to move faster.

Buck wanted to reach for him, but Aiden was pulling on Buck.

"Gotta go. Gotta go now," Aiden screamed in Buck's ear. "It sees us."

Buck turned around and saw Bigfoot heading down quickly.

Mario got to the ridge and Buck was able to pull him up.

Bigfoot let out a howl that nearly paralyzed Buck.

"Gotta go," Aiden kept saying over and over.

CHAPTER NINETEEN

Buck, Aiden and Mario were running toward the three-wheeler while Bigfoot was on a crash course for them, heading down the mountain.

"Hurry and get on," Buck said.

"How?" Aiden asked.

Buck got on and started the trike.

Mario tried to push past Aiden but he was too weak. Aiden got on and scooted as close to Buck as he could. Mario had only a thin sliver of the seat and was gripping not only Aiden but Buck's shoulders, too.

Buck took off, aware Bigfoot was nearly to them. He hoped the monster couldn't outrun a three-wheeler.

Throwing caution to the wind, Buck opened it up and flew down the trail, hoping they wouldn't crash into a tree or hit a rock that might upend them. He was also aware anything jarring might throw all three of them off the trike.

The sound of crashing trees rose behind them, and even with the engine revving Buck could still hear the monster right behind them.

He zipped around a curve and the front wheel was off the ground for a few hazardous seconds, Buck holding his breath and leaning to get the trike back onto the rough trail.

Aiden was shouting in his ear but there was too much noise for Buck to make out any of the words. Aiden might also be losing his cool and screaming blindly, too.

Buck didn't know how Mario was faring but knew he was still back there because of the awkward weight. The trike wasn't handling as well as it usually did, but it was all they had right now.

He careened over some loose dirt and the front wheel caught for a second, just enough for Buck to lose control, his hands flying off and briefly no one steering the trike. He overcorrected and skimmed the mountainside, ripping at his pant leg.

He heard Aiden and Mario both scream as they were caught between a rock and a hard place as well, but then there was a clear path down several hundred feet that Buck was glad to see.

Risking an accident, he put pedal to the metal and focused on getting the trike and all three of the occupants to the camp in one piece.

He didn't know if Bigfoot was right behind them or had dropped off, finally, but he wasn't going to chance looking back. Better to be pleasantly surprised when he got back and saw Bigfoot had given up.

Even if Bigfoot followed them into camp, it was better to be surprised at the end and die, rather than knowing it was coming the entire trip.

At least Buck tried to see it that way. He knew he needed to stay focused on the trail ahead and not worry about everything else, which he could not control.

The trail was nearly a flat, straight track, like he was on a course. Buck slowed down at the next turn, which was almost a ninety degree angle, and managed a glance over his shoulder.

Bigfoot was still back there but further up the trail than when they'd started their descent.

Buck didn't want to chance anything so he kept up the fast pace, only braking when he absolutely had to. More often than not he was veering slightly off the well-worn trail but not enough to spill.

Aiden was yelling in his ear again, but Buck shook his head. He needed to concentrate.

The trike was shaking from side to side as they moved, and Buck hoped it wasn't out of fuel or had a problem. He didn't want to take his eyes off the trail to see if there were any lights on the gauges.

Buck didn't recognize anywhere he was driving, but it had been dark going the other way, and without Bigfoot in pursuit.

They weren't that far up the mountain now. Buck thought he knew where they were. Not on the same trail they'd started on but maybe close enough.

He raced past two workers, picking marijuana in a field.

Buck wanted to stop and tell them to run but couldn't risk stopping.

Both workers stopped and stared. Buck yelled but knew it was lost on the wind. They'd likely think Buck was out joyriding on the trike.

Around the next bend there were small grow fields on either side but Buck didn't see more workers. He knew generally where he was and decided to slow down.

As awful as it sounded, if Bigfoot was still in pursuit he'd go after the low-hanging fruit of the two workers.

Unfortunately, he was right. He could hear the screams as the engine idled.

"Go, bro. What are you doing?" Aiden yelled.

Buck nodded and took off at a safer speed.

Mario was still quiet back there.

They traveled back to the camp and Buck parked in front of Gestapo Karl's cabin.

"Where have you been?" Gestapo Karl stepped outside and stretched. He looked like he'd been napping. "Where's the rest of ya? And the stupid brothers?"

Mario frowned. "Man, have we got a story to tell."

Gestapo Karl was staring at Buck. "Why were you driving and where are my other two three-wheelers?"

"One is over the cliff and the other we left behind," Buck said.

Gestapo Karl looked angry. "I'm going to need you idiots to go back up and get my trike. I paid for those myself. I also have my bosses coming up the mountain any minute, so get inside and we need to make this quick."

Mario turned to Buck and Aiden. "You two stay outside. I can explain it."

Buck and Aiden exchanged glances.

"I don't think so," Buck said. "Gestapo Karl will only get half of the story, and I have a feeling you'll paint yourself as a hero in all of this, when we saved your life."

"What did you just call me, moron?"

Buck sighed. He was exhausted. "I called you Gestapo Karl. Everyone calls you that. As if you didn't already know. I'm guessing you publicly don't want it used because you like to think everyone is scared of you."

Gestapo Karl smiled. "Are you saying you're not scared, maggot?"

Buck shrugged. "I was very afraid of you... until Bigfoot tried to kill me, like he did everyone not standing here, sir."

Not far from where they were standing rose a howling.

Bigfoot was at the base of the mountain and likely wreaking havoc among the workers in the fields.

"Time to get inside," Gestapo Karl said.

CHAPTER TWENTY

Karl closed and locked the door, going to the window and making sure it was also latched. "Tell me what happened, and no crap. No lies. No making yourself look good."

"We went up the mountain and lost a guy as we approached the cave," Mario said. "Bigfoot snatched him right off a trike."

Mario explained the rest of it, up until Buck and Aiden had to go into the cave, but Mario claimed they volunteered.

"Not true. We were forced in," Buck said.

Karl pointed at Aiden. "You tell me what happened in the cave and then we'll get back to Mario's version of things."

Aiden nodded. "We wandered inside. Didn't find those two guys but found a natural water source and a lot of bones around it. Animals and maybe humans. Then we kept going and there was a deep, dark hole and couldn't go further. We got totally lost and wandered for hours, until we found some old mine cars and tracks and followed them up until we were out of the mountain. We found the trikes but decided on using only one. Less targets."

Karl was still looking out the window. He didn't see anything amiss and wondered if he should call everyone back in, but then his bosses would know there was something wrong.

He did not want to annoy the bosses, because they'd be quick to replace him.

Karl put his hand up and pointed at Mario. "Your turn."

"Bigfoot attacked us. Killed the other guy I was with. Forced me off the side of the mountain, where I managed at the last second to grab onto a tree and climb to safety," Mario said.

"Not true. We found and rescued him," Aiden said.

Mario rolled his eyes. "Whatever."

"You're here and alive, so I don't really care how it happened," Karl said and pointed at Buck. "Finish the story."

"I raced down the mountain with Bigfoot in pursuit. He was right behind us but then we saw two workers in a field and Bigfoot stopped and killed them, I guess. We didn't stop to find out. Then… here we are." Buck was also looking out of the window, standing next to Karl.

Karl sighed. "If Bigfoot gets into camp we're all dead. You know that, right?"

"We need to evacuate. Pull everyone inside and lock the doors," Buck said. "Do we have weapons to pass out?"

Karl chuckled. "I'm not giving loaded weapons to this group. Buncha potheads and simpletons with guns? I'd rather take my chances with Bigfoot."

"We need to do something." Buck pointed. "I see dust."

Karl groaned. "The bosses are here. We need to act like this is business as usual. Got it? I'll give them an excuse, we saw someone in an upper field walking around and so I'll pull everyone closer to camp for a day or so and tell him we have a large group searching for this trespasser. That usually works."

"Have you had to do this in the past?" Buck asked.

"I can't imagine this is the first time Bigfoot has gotten too close." Aiden was shaking.

Karl nodded. "Every now and then some idiot will go up the mountain and poke the bear, as they say."

"Then why send us up there?" Buck asked.

"First of all, don't you worry about what I command. Secondly, I wanted you idiots to find the other idiots before Bigfoot got mad and went on a rampage." Karl was fuming. He didn't owe an explanation to this nobody.

A black SUV pulled up in front of Karl's cabin and six men got out and looked around.

Karl groaned. He did not need this today of all days. "Everyone act cool. Hopefully I can get them out of here earlier than usual. They might leave before nightfall, if we're lucky."

He walked outside and made sure to smile. "Welcome, gentlemen. I hope your trip was uneventful."

Karl was listening for the telltale sounds of Bigfoot, either killing his workers or growling, as he approached. If he decided to rip the camp apart there wasn't much anyone could do.

I'll need to pull out both shotguns and every weapon hidden in my office and all the ammo, Karl thought.

He wondered how he'd do it if he had to wine and dine these boss idiots, though.

If they got wind of anything wrong they'd pull the plug on the entire operation. Karl knew he was valuable but not irreplaceable. They'd simply pull up stakes and find another part of the mountain or another mountain completely to set this all back up, hiring someone else to take his place.

"We'll walk around a bit and call you when we're ready for a report," Hans, the big boss, said, waving dismissively at Karl.

"Excellent. I await your further instruction." Karl went back inside his cabin. The three idiots were still inside. "Listen up. I need radio silence about Bigfoot. Got it?" He pointed at Mario. "Take a man loyal to you, to us, and find out if the workers are dead or not. Bury them if you have to. We'll figure out who they are and all that later."

"What about us?" Buck asked.

"I need you two to find higher ground and keep watch. If you see the monster, call me." Karl went to his desk and pulled out a burner phone. He never gave them out to anyone, including guys like Mario who were supposedly loyal. He figured this was as good a time as any to use the phones. "I'm the only number listed and you shouldn't be able to call off the mountain."

Karl took out a pair of Glocks from another drawer and made sure they were loaded. "Can you two morons fire a gun?"

Buck and Aiden both nodded.

"Good. Casually walk out and find a good spot to see the upper fields. I don't want any surprises today," Karl said.

The three idiots were still in his cabin.

Karl forced himself not to scream and alert the bosses something was wrong. "Go. Now. Stay away from the owners. Get going."

He watched as they ran off. Karl stood in front of his cabin and hoped nothing else bad was going to happen. With any luck, Bigfoot would be satisfied for now.

It didn't matter if he decided tomorrow would be the day to kill every last person in camp.

Karl needed the monster to get lost for a few hours, go back to his cave and snack on the multiple men he'd killed already in the last day or so.

Hopefully, us going up there won't get him too mad, since he's eating, Karl thought.

CHAPTER TWENTY-ONE

Buck found a spot between the camp and the fields, so he could see everything coming and going. Aiden was antsy so Buck told him to sneak back into camp and find them food and water. They hadn't had anything in nearly a day.

I wish I had a pair of binoculars, Buck thought. He would be able to see and cover much more ground. *If Aiden gets restless again I'll send him back for a pair.*

There was movement in one of the far fields but it was too far to see what it was. Could be a man standing on a trike, could be one of the pickup trucks they used to transport product, could be Bigfoot crouching down and ready to kill.

Buck saw Gestapo Karl walking near the closest field to the camp, an echo of his boisterous words on the wind.

Did we show Karl we could be trusted? He's given us a better job than the trenches, Buck thought. *With any luck, this will hold even after the bosses are long gone.* Maybe he'd even ask Buck and Aiden to lead a large group of well-armed men back to the caves to rid the mountain once and for all of the monster. Imagine how much a Bigfoot body could fetch.

Buck shook his head. Even if they killed it, no way would anyone want the world to know where it was living. The mountain would be swarming with idiots and their cryptid groups.

They weren't wrong, though, were they? There really is a cryptid living in California, Buck thought.

If the rumors were true, it had been here a very long time. Generations of growers had seen it or seen clues about it still being alive. It might live to be hundreds of years old.

Buck wondered where it came from and if it had been provoked in the past to take action.

Maybe it was back in the caves with all the new bodies, sleeping it off. Doing whatever Bigfoot did. Having a good, long nap with a full belly.

More movement coming up but Buck saw it was only Aiden. His friend looked tired.

"I scrounged a couple of salami sandwiches and a gallon of water," Aiden said and dropped down next to Buck. "I am tired, bro."

"Sleep."

Aiden shook his head. "No way. We're supposed to be on watch for the creature."

"Only one of us needs to be awake," Buck said. "Power nap. Then one of us needs to find some binoculars. It will help cover more ground."

Aiden nodded and bit into a sandwich. He sighed. "I never tasted a better salami sandwich."

Buck joined him and agreed.

"We really could've died up there." Buck was trying not to think about it, but the simple fact of being able to bite into a sandwich had his thoughts running all over the place.

"Yes, and the giant gold ball would never be found again, maybe," Aiden said. "We need to figure out a way to get it down the mountain to my van."

To Buck that was important but not high on the list right now. Survival was a big one. Making sure they never ran into Bigfoot again, too.

He finished his sandwich and drank a lot of water, staring out and trying not to fall asleep.

Aiden was snoring softly next to him within a few minutes.

Buck smiled. Despite the few bumps they'd had in the last couple of days, he'd do anything for Aiden. They were friends forever. Buck's only real friend, too.

Sitting here, without a joint to pass between them, as sober as they'd been in years, Buck had a new understanding of their friendship. They were going to be the other person growing up together, no matter what. A ride or die friendship.

If we survive this summer, Buck thought. He wasn't just talking about being around one another and seeing how far the friendship could stretch before breaking, he meant actual survival.

Not being ripped apart and eaten by a legendary monster no one knew existed. Really, truly existed. Except him, Aiden and Mario.

Buck wondered how Mario was faring. Not that he liked the guy, but they'd been through a harrowing escape. There had to be a bond there, even if it was tenuous.

Gestapo Karl and his bosses were moving back toward the camp, which was probably a good thing. They needed to stay inside and not in the open, where Bigfoot could rush them and likely slice through half of them before there was a scream.

It was several hours before dark. Buck wondered how long they were supposed to stay out here. Would Gestapo Karl relieve them and send out two new people?

Buck doubted it. He supposed they'd be out here until the camp started to settle down and then sneak back in, grab some dinner and pray no one died tonight.

If he saw Mario or Gestapo Karl he'd ask them what else needed to be done. If he was seen, actually. Buck's goal was to get a good night's sleep and hope Bigfoot was back to hiding in his cave.

Buck kept watch but didn't see anything out of the ordinary. No Bigfoot, no alien spacecraft, no Loch Ness Monster in the water tanks. Just another beautiful day on the mountainside with endless fields of marijuana to admire.

Aiden snored for another hour before he stirred and sat up.

"Get enough sleep?" Buck asked.

Aiden shrugged. "I'll take over. Anything I need to know about?"

"I think the three guys in the field on the left are stealing a couple of plants, but otherwise… no one has been ripped apart by Bigfoot in a few hours." Buck put his head in some weeds and got as comfortable as he could. "Wake me in a couple of hours."

Buck felt like he closed his eyes for a second before Aiden shook him awake.

"The bosses are doing something," Aiden said.

Buck sat up. It took him a second for his eyes to adjust.

Gestapo Karl was standing next to the SUV, holding the door open as the bosses milled about talking.

"They're leaving," Buck said, wishing it to be true. "Get in and drive away."

It would be dark within the hour. If they were going to leave, now would be a perfect time. They'd have enough light left to drive down the mountain safely.

Safe from the night and a wrong turn down the dirt road.

Safe from a Bigfoot attack. If it was coming it would come in the middle of the night.

Aiden groaned and Buck shook his head.

One of the bosses closed the SUV door without getting inside.

Gestapo Karl did not look happy as he led the men to his cabin.

They were going to spend the night.

CHAPTER TWENTY-TWO

Karl wanted to scream. He'd tried to coax the bosses to leave so they could find a good hotel for the night. Come back in the morning to see the operation in full motion again, or get on a plane and fly back to wherever they came from.

His cabin only had two cots in it. Karl would need to kick his management team out of their cabins, although it would be easier since a few of them had died at the Bigfoot cave.

"I'll have the men bring you food, I guess," Karl said. He'd told the cooks to make something decent tonight because there was always a chance the bosses would stay. About every third or fourth summer they visited they stayed at the camp. Thought they were being one of the guys and hanging out, as if these workers wanted to hobnob with upper management.

Karl knew they mostly disliked him. How would they feel about these six men? They hated them, Karl was certain. Why wouldn't they? When Karl had first started, all those years ago, he'd been a nobody like everyone else in camp. He'd hated all of these men for years but now he was directly working for them. He knew their rules were stupid and if they'd once listened to Karl's ideas they'd make a lot more money each season.

But no, they knew better. Even though none of them had ever gotten their hands dirty. Never figured out how to properly raise a plant, how to make it into a potent drug. How to do anything in the field. They thought they knew how to sell and market it, but Karl knew they were behind the times.

With marijuana legal and dispensaries popping up on every corner, it was harder to sell to the customers. They were all quickly getting a doctor's note so they could buy regulated weed, with pretty names and strains, rich flavors added to them.

It wasn't about the high anymore. It was about being a hipster. Looking cool in front of your loser friends.

Karl knew at some point in the near future this operation would be shut down. Even the Feds didn't bother them anymore, too busy going after the illegal manufacturing of edibles. Much easier to take down since it was all happening within miles of their cop shops and not up a friggin' mountain.

These bosses either didn't understand what was happening or didn't really care. They seemed like they were going through the motions, too, not even paying attention as Karl showed them around another summer.

Most of them had their phones out, trying to get a signal they'd never get up here.

Karl wondered why they were even here, and so early in the season, too. Usually they waited until the end so they could let him know what he needed to do to keep pace with last year's numbers, or pat him on the back because he was way ahead.

He was never behind because he already knew where he stood and what the numbers were. Once the weed got off the mountain and into the hands of the suppliers, Karl couldn't care less. He knew what needed to be harvested. He knew what needed to be done for job security.

The bosses had no clue about Bigfoot. Karl had made sure they never found out, because they seemed like they'd be scared off easily. In all these years they'd never had anything more than a few missing workers. Par for the course. Not that big a deal. Most of these workers were homeless druggy bums. No one would miss them and no one knew exactly where they were, either.

Karl told the bosses he'd be back to make more room for them tonight and stepped outside. It would be dark in minutes. He'd already pulled everyone back from the fields and made sure there were a few old-timers with weapons hiding inside the compound.

He wanted no surprises tonight.

The last thing he needed was an incident, big or small. He knew he was being paranoid, but this visit didn't feel like any of the others in the past. The bosses didn't ask many questions and ignored most of what Karl was asking them.

He'd sent Mario to see if those other two guys were still watching and if they needed anything, although he'd let Mario know they were to head back inside once dinner started, before dark.

Karl needed this night to go smoothly. It felt like a tall order right now, though, with a very large and scary unknown somewhere out there.

He found the six men beds they could use, finding Mario sleeping in his bed.

"Get up and get lost. The bosses are staying and want the bed," Karl had told Mario.

"Where am I supposed to sleep?"

"In the barracks with the others." Karl stared at Mario, waiting for an argument, but Mario sighed and grabbed his things.

Before Mario was out the door, Karl stopped him. "Hey, did you get those two back inside?"

Mario nodded. "They were chicken and heading back already."

Karl knew they'd been brave in the last twenty-four hours, while Mario had nearly been killed. Mario owed his life to those two chickens, but decided not to say anything.

He would once the bosses left, though.

The bosses were shown to their quarters and they didn't look happy.

What do you want me to do, huh? Your cheapness paid for this camp, and you wouldn't ever give me any money to upgrade, so here you go, Karl thought.

None of the bosses openly complained but Karl could see the looks they were passing quietly.

"We'll need to use your office for the next couple of hours," the head boss said. "Bring us food, too. Any chance you have any spirits?"

Karl had quite a few bottles of bourbon and rum hidden in his closet but nodded slowly. "I might have a bottle tucked away. I usually open it the last day we're in camp, before we start the next growing season."

"Bring it with the food."

Karl went to the mess hall and frowned. They were cooking cheeseburgers, fries and tater tots.

"I told you to make something good tonight. Fancy. What's this picnic crap?" Karl was mad.

The cooks all shrugged. "We don't have steak and lobster. This was the fanciest we had. Unless you'd rather have fried chicken, but then we'd need to thaw the chicken."

Karl felt like he was going to explode, but it wasn't the cooks' fault. It was the six cheap men currently in his office. "Make them as fancy as you can. I'll need food for the bosses right away."

"We are almost done," a cook said. "The men are lined up and ready."

Karl saw the line and shook his head. "I don't care about them. They eat once the bosses get their food."

"As you wish," a cook said.

"Bring it to my office and put it on a tray or something so it's not a bunch of paper plates with burgers on it. Okay?" Karl wanted to scream. This was not going well so far.

He rushed back to his cabin, shuddering when he heard a distant roar. He could lie to himself and say it was a mountain lion, but he knew what it really was.

Stay away tonight, Karl thought. *Just give me one more peaceful night.*

CHAPTER TWENTY-THREE

"We need to make sure we're in the center of the barracks tonight," Buck said. He was talking to Aiden, behind him in line.

"We need to get away from this mountain." Aiden was shaking. Despite getting a bit of sleep, he looked dazed. Confused.

Buck shuffled forward in line. He was very hungry and saw there were cheeseburgers and fries, which he enjoyed. Who didn't, right?

"Keep the line moving," someone behind them yelled.

Buck realized he was also in a daze and hadn't moved up, leaving a big gap between him and the back of the guy in front of him. He walked forward.

Mario walked up and stepped in front of Buck. When someone said something behind them in line, Mario laughed. "Do you forget who I am, idiot? If you're man enough, step up and drag me out of line."

No one said a word.

"I didn't think so." Mario glanced at Buck and Aiden. "You two look awful."

"We slept on a rock," Aiden said.

Mario chuckled. "I got thrown out of my cabin. Looks like I'm sleeping with the common trash like you two."

"Lucky us," Buck said.

They got to the front and Mario pointed at Buck and Aiden. "These two are with me, so they get the good burgers and double fries and tots. Got it?"

Buck didn't want to ask why Mario was being so nice, but couldn't help himself. "Are we all buddies now?"

Mario chuckled again. "No, but I need you two sharper than you are right now. I think we have a long night ahead of us. Don't you?"

Buck nodded. He had a really bad feeling about tonight. They'd be trapped in the barracks with dozens of other men. If Bigfoot decided to crash the party there would be utter chaos. People would be heading for the exits, crushing together.

An easy mass target for the monster.

"Is there anywhere else we can go?" Aiden asked.

Mario nodded. "There is one place we can try to hide, but it won't be comfortable. If we're seen we're dead, too. Six of one, half a dozen of the other, I guess."

"If Bigfoot attacks the barracks everyone will likely die," Buck said.

"Agreed." Mario went to the farthest bench, putting his food tray down and telling the three guys already seated there to get lost. They stood and found another table.

"Where are you talking about?" Aiden asked.

Mario pointed toward the kitchen. "There's an old office in the back of the mess hall. Never used except when Gestapo Karl wants us to take care of a problem, if you know what I mean."

Buck knew what he meant, and thought, if things had kept going as they'd started, Aiden and himself might have been taken there and roughed up. Or worse.

"There's only one window and it's covered in paper, so no one can see inside. We drag some sleeping bags, food and weapons and camp there tonight," Mario said.

"What access in and out is there?" Buck asked.

"The back door to the kitchen but it will be bolted at night. The cooks should be cleaning and leaving in a couple of hours, but I have a key." Mario took a bite of his burger and smiled. "Not bad tonight. You don't want to know what the rest of these idiots are really eating. There might be some meat actually mixed in."

Buck didn't want to know what they'd been fed so far. "Then what do we do for the next couple of hours?"

"We watch and wait. I'll need you two to go to the barracks as soon as we're done eating and grab pillows and blankets. I'll get the guns. We have all the food we can eat, and I might have a surprise or two," Mario said.

The trio ate quickly and rushed off to do their tasks.

Buck and Aiden were in the barracks, grabbing their pillows and blankets, when a couple of the other workers started to watch them.

"We need a cover story," Aiden said.

"I got this. Keep going and grab for Mario, too." Buck had his pillows and blankets in hand. He watched as the two men walked over to him.

"Where are you two weasels sleeping tonight, huh?" The taller of the two smiled. "With each other?"

The other man laughed, showing off his broken teeth.

"Yes, as a matter of fact we are. Do you have a problem with it? Gestapo Karl doesn't. In fact, he told us to grab our things and leave." Buck took a deep breath, hoping his supposed admission would startle these two enough to get out.

"No way. Uh uh," the man stammered.

Aiden went up to Buck and kissed his cheek. "Come on, lover. Time to head home and be our true selves."

Buck pushed past the guy but heard the two men following. They were whispering and he heard a couple of crude words about their sexuality.

"This isn't going to work," Aiden said.

Buck got to the door. They needed to hurry. It was dark outside and going to get darker by the minute. They needed to be in place so they could get into the mess hall as soon as the cooks were done cleaning up.

"Hey, wait a minute, both of you," the man said, adding a few insults.

"No time. Gotta leave or Gestapo Karl is going to be mad," Buck said. He opened the door. "Unless you want to be fired, too. We could easily say you're with us, if you know what I mean. Up to you. Done working already this summer?"

The two men looked annoyed.

Buck walked out and Aiden quickly followed. They ran across the camp, ignoring anyone looking in their direction.

They rounded the mess hall and stopped near the small shed out back for dry goods, leaning against the wall within sight of the open back door to the kitchen.

Buck could hear pots and pans being banged around, men joking and laughing.

"Now what?" Aiden asked.

Buck looked around. There were no lights back here, only the thin light from the back door. "We keep an eye out for an attack, and we wait for Mario."

CHAPTER TWENTY-FOUR

Karl tried to keep smiling, even as the words sunk in.

I'm losing my job. This is it. Our last season. These guys don't even care, Karl thought.

They'd eaten their cheeseburgers in his office, crowded around his desk. Karl finished his food quickly but the bosses took a bite or two and piled the plates onto his desk.

Then they hit him with the real reason they were here.

Karl nodded stupidly as they told him what they'd just figured out, what he'd known for a long time: illegal weed sales were way down because every idiot had access to the internet and how to grow your own in your house. Street pot was cheap and everywhere. Those people too lazy got a medical card so they could buy it openly and freely.

"So… what about me?" Karl finally asked.

The bosses were all smiling.

"We'll have something for you to do after this summer. Promise."

Karl could see the lie in their eyes. They'd toss him out and move on to whatever their new plans were going to be.

I should walk out now. It would be the smart thing to do, Karl thought.

Except he knew there was a Bigfoot lurking nearby, and he was sure it would attack tonight. Sure this conversation might be moot.

"How do I know you're not jerking my chain, stringing me along for the next few weeks, and then you'll tell me to get lost?" Karl asked, reaching for the bottle of bourbon on the desk.

Everyone had had two finger pours of the bourbon. It wasn't even the good stuff. Karl was going to save that for himself.

If he survived the night he'd take the alcohol with him when he rode a trike down to his vehicle in the morning and leave these men to deal with the camp.

The head boss smiled and took out an envelope from his pocket. "This is a retainer of sorts. So that you don't leave until the end of summer. Every week we'll give you another envelope, and then a generous severance package on the last day. Does that sound fair? We'll still want to retain you for what we're doing in the future."

"And what is that?" Karl asked.

"We've struck a deal with a specific cartel from Colombia. They will supply us with product and we will distribute it from our warehouses all over California."

Karl shook his head. "Two problems I see immediately. Dealing with a drug cartel is a bad move, and being close to civilization is also bad. The government will get wind of it and we'll all be arrested."

"No. We have already made inroads with law enforcement. We will have protection as long as we ship the product out of state."

Karl sighed. This was going from bad to worse. "And what if I want to retire and not have to deal with a cartel?"

"Then you take your severance and you go your own way."

Karl knew they'd never let him leave. If he wasn't part of their new scheme he'd be a liability. They'd have him killed. He wondered if they'd hire someone to shoot him, to blow up his truck or make it look like a suicide. With these bosses, it felt like nothing was off the table.

"What cartel? Can you tell me? I'd like to know who I'll be working with." Karl finished the last of his fries and piled his plate on top of the others.

The bosses shared another glance, as if these morons had some secret silent code or could read each other's minds.

I can read their minds. It's all filled with money and scheming and garbage, Karl thought.

"The Orenato Cartel is our new partner."

Karl nodded slowly, taking it in. He knew them by name. He'd never dealt with anyone from the organization. They were big time drug dealers, sending cocaine as their main product but dabbling in everything else, too. Trafficking. Meth. Pills. Edibles.

But not weed as far as Karl knew. The Orenato Cartel had long ago figured out they could get a much bigger profit on anything else. Weed was so five minutes ago to them.

Karl needed to play it cool. He also wanted to count the money in the envelope and see how much they were going to bonus him weekly. It might be a good move to stay on, skim much more weed than he usually did, and collect until it was all gone.

The first week there isn't an envelope or I get an excuse about it, I'm going to load up my truck with as much of this product as I can and tell the workers what's really happening and hope they tear the place apart, Karl thought.

He'd definitely take more weed and see whatever else he could steal between now and September, too. He'd have Mario help him but not tell him, because he was afraid Mario would take it too far himself and steal too much or let others know.

One of the bosses leaned forward and frowned. "What are you thinking about, Karl? Something that we won't be pleased about?"

"No. Of course not," Karl lied.

"That's all for tonight. We are going to turn in. We have a long day ahead of us tomorrow. A long drive."

Karl stood and grabbed the plates. He wanted to throw them in their faces, but decided he'd be cool. For now.

He also toyed with the idea of alerting the Feds or the ATF about the camp, once it got close to the end. Karl didn't really care about all of the losers who worked under him. They knew the risks.

Karl was going to maximize his profits and his take from this camp before he left.

He was truly worried about working with a drug cartel from Colombia, too. They could be ruthless and Karl knew one false move, one stupid word, and he'd be dead.

It wasn't worth the risk to Karl.

He left his cabin and tried to remain calm, but it was really dark outside. There was too much cloud cover and he couldn't see more than a few feet in front of him. He used the few lights in the camp to make his way to the barracks.

Mario would be there and they could find a quiet corner and hope the Bigfoot didn't attack them.

Karl had three pistols hidden on his body and enough ammo to kill half of the workers.

He hoped it would be enough to take down Bigfoot, or at least slow the creature down so he could escape.

Karl stopped at the barracks door and opened the envelope.

He counted the money and smiled. Five thousand dollars was more than he made in two weeks.

Maybe he'd stay on a little longer.

CHAPTER TWENTY-FIVE

Buck sat up. He'd been nearly asleep and thought he heard a howl, but it could've only been in his dream.

Mario was at the window. He'd cut a small hole in the paper and was seated on a bar stool so he could see out without having to shift too much.

Aiden was snoring softly on his blanket.

Mario nodded when he saw Buck looking at him. "You heard it too, right?"

"Yes. How far off was it?" Buck sat up. He wondered if he should wake Aiden yet but thought better of it. The more sleep they got the better.

"I thought I saw movement but can't be sure. If it was Bigfoot, he's definitely in camp. Over near my cabin," Mario said.

Buck was scared. "If Bigfoot starts attacking, what do we do?"

Mario shook his head. "Nothing. We stay put and see what happens. Hopefully it will run itself ragged attacking everyone else. Maybe a few workers will run off into the woods and Bigfoot will need to run after them, hunt them down and rip them apart. That might be taxing on it. I dunno. Leaving this room is crazy unless it finds us."

Buck had to agree. There was nowhere truly safe in camp, but being exposed outside or with all of the workers in the barracks made no sense.

"Make sure your weapon is loaded and the safety is off," Mario said. "We shoot to kill. Anything we see coming near us gets all of our firepower."

Buck didn't know if he agreed with that thought for a couple of reasons. "What if it's a worker trying to escape, or someone else who heard the howl and is out investigating?"

Mario grinned. "Then he's going to be out of luck. There can't be any hesitation on our part." He went back to the window.

Buck paced the small room. He didn't like any of this, but knew it was dog eat dog now. If Bigfoot attacked they needed to fight fire with fire.

And every other cliche, Buck thought.

"Take over for a second, I gotta go hit the head," Mario said.

"I didn't think there were bathrooms in the mess hall."

Mario shrugged. "There are sinks."

"Gross."

"You'll be changing your mind when it's time for you to take care of your own stuff. I'll knock lightly three times, so you know it's me," Mario said.

Mario slipped out and Aiden rolled over and groaned.

Buck went to his friend, who woke up with a start. "I had a bad dream. We were being chased by a monster."

"I'm afraid that's our reality," Buck said. "If you'd told me a couple of days ago we'd be hiding out so Bigfoot didn't eat us, I'd think you were nuts or high."

"I'd give anything to be high," Aiden said.

"Might not be a good idea, all things considered… but maybe for a few minutes so I didn't have a heart attack with all of the stress." Buck went to the window and peeked out but he couldn't see anything.

"Where's Mario?" Aiden asked.

"Going to the bathroom in a sink." Buck smiled at Aiden, although he thought it might be too dark to see the expression. "If you need to go, wait for him to come back. He's going to knock lightly three times so we don't shoot him."

Aiden chuckled. "I'm not sure that's such a bad thing. He got us into this mess. Right?"

"I guess. We could blame him or Gestapo Karl for sending us in the first place, but I think at some point, whoever went up the mountain was going to piss the creature off." Buck thought he saw movement back toward the barracks but it was too dark and too far to get a good read.

Three knocks on the door before it was opened and Mario stepped back inside. He had an unopened box of Oreo cookies with him. "Found this in Gestapo Karl's secret storage spot. You gotta see all the snacks he has in there."

Mario sat on the floor and opened the cookies, passing it around after taking a handful for himself.

"Anything out there?" Mario asked.

Buck sighed. "I don't know. It's too dark. My eyes and brain might be messing with me, but I thought I saw something, but only briefly."

"Then we sit and eat cookies until daylight," Mario said.

Buck figured they had a few hours until it would be light enough to attempt an escape. If they could get on a trike and get to Aiden's van, they'd have a chance of living.

"Maybe we should pack some food and water and whatever else we need, so when it's time to get off the mountain we'll have supplies," Buck said.

"Good idea, but we can't make too much noise." Mario shoved two Oreos in his mouth. "I'll get everything since I know where it is."

Buck figured out what he was saying with his mouth full of cookies.

Mario pointed at the window. "One of you needs to keep an eye out there. We need to make sure there's nothing in the back for when we make our run."

"I got it," Aiden said and sat on the stool.

Buck stood in the doorway when Mario left. They didn't need to keep the door closed right now. Buck also wanted to make sure he could keep an eye on Mario so he didn't leave them behind.

"I don't trust him," Aiden said, as if reading Buck's mind. "Do you?"

Buck shook his head. "What's that expression your dad always said?"

"I trust you as far as I can throw you." Aiden chuckled. "It makes sense now."

"Yes, it certainly does." Buck watched as Mario moved around the kitchen, filling a few brown paper bags and plastic bags with items.

Buck went back inside the room and stood next to Aiden, ripping another small hole in the paper over the window. He wanted to see outside as well, fearing they'd be attacked at any moment.

Mario dropped something heavy in the kitchen at the same exact second Buck and Aiden both gasped.

Something very big was only a few feet from where they were hiding, and Buck was sure a giant Bigfoot head turned in their direction.

CHAPTER TWENTY-SIX

The first attack came so suddenly no one had time to sit up in their bunk before three men had been slashed across their necks or eviscerated.

Karl sat up and immediately rolled off his bed, hitting the floor and reaching under his pillow above for his weapons.

I should've handed out guns, Karl thought. No time for any of that now.

He heard a cracking sound and part of the wall next to him was demolished as Bigfoot tore through the wood like it was tissue paper. He grabbed a man out of his bed and bit clean through his neck, tearing an arm off for good measure.

Everyone was running for the exits but Bigfoot, despite his size, was too fast.

Karl could see the glint of the claws as Bigfoot began methodically wading through the frightened, screaming workers, slicing them to pieces as he moved.

He remembered a friend he grew up with, Mo, who used to have piranha as pets. The real ones from the Amazon and not those fake red-belly things they sold at the pet store.

The piranha wouldn't eat everything in the tank with them all at once. They weren't like dogs. When Mo would dump a few dozen goldfish in with the piranha, they'd swarm the goldfish and bite off their fins, leaving the goldfish unable to swim away.

Then the piranha would eat one or two each per day, their food floating helplessly.

To Karl it felt like Bigfoot was doing the same, staying low and slicing Achilles tendons, making sure his prey couldn't run away from him.

By the time he got to the door, everyone was moaning and on the floor. Bigfoot stepped on a few of them as he turned and ran to the other door, where only a few people had escaped.

Karl stayed where he was, hoping it was too dark for the monster to see him, or maybe he'd be more interested in a group of people instead of one cowering under a bed.

Bigfoot burst from the barracks, tearing part of the wall and the door as he drove through it like a linebacker.

Karl didn't need to know what was happening, and knew Bigfoot would be back for him soon enough. He slid out from under the bed, made sure he had all of his weapons, and rushed out of the other door.

The bosses were standing near his cabin, looking confused.

Bigfoot howled, not too far from where they stood.

"Run, you stupid idiots," Karl said as he ran past the bosses. He had no idea where he was going to go, though. If he tried to stumble down the mountain he'd fall and get hurt, or make too much noise and be the new target.

Better to find a better place to hide.

One of the bosses was shouting for Karl to stop, but then he was cut off and screamed.

Karl knew the bosses were all going to die, and he didn't feel bad about it. Not much. It was kill or be killed, and he knew Bigfoot was a killing machine.

What was the old adage about facing a hungry bear in the forest? To make sure you weren't the slowest person, Karl thought.

Behind his cabin was a natural rock outcropping with a small hole through it on ground level. Karl knew he couldn't completely fit inside of it, but he could keep an eye out for an attack.

He got into position and had his weapons in hand as he got down on his stomach.

The bosses were all dead, torn apart. Even with hardly any moonlight, Karl could smell the carnage. He could see the unmoving shapes of the men scattered near his cabin.

Men were screaming in the distance, but Karl knew it wasn't safe to come out of hiding. For whatever reason, he wondered where Mario was hiding. Not that he necessarily liked the guy, but maybe he had a better spot.

Karl saw a large shape moving left to right, past his cabin, but it blended into shadows.

He heard another roar but under the rock it echoed and he couldn't get a sense of how close it truly was.

I'm losing it, Karl thought. He was shaking. He wiped sweat from his face and tried to focus on the darkness.

Someone ran past his hiding spot, only a few feet away.

In seconds he heard the person scream and what sounded like a body hitting the ground.

Bigfoot was in the vicinity. Karl held his breath.

Now it was quiet. Had Bigfoot killed everyone so quickly, or were some workers able to hide for the moment? Karl wasn't moving until he absolutely had to.

He tried to burrow deeper into the rock hole but it was no use. Half of his body was sticking out but this was better than running blindly and falling off a cliff.

If I get out of this alive, I'm going to live a better life, Karl thought.

He didn't know what that really meant but he'd figure it all out once he got to safety. Maybe he could go on the news channels and tell everyone about the attack and how he was the only survivor. How he'd bravely fought off Bigfoot and escaped.

The part where he was the boss of an illegal marijuana grow zone was going to need to be glossed over. He'd have time to make up a story. Maybe he was here against his will. None of the bosses were alive to argue against any story he told.

Karl thought he might be a hero. If nothing else, he could go on that weird cryptid dude's show he saw on cable every now and then. Hunter Shaya? Was that his name?

The pressure on his ankle was so slight at first Karl thought a large bug or maybe a snake was back there.

He tried to move his leg but he was held firmer now, and Karl tried to grab onto the rock somewhere as he was yanked out so violently he lost one of the guns.

Karl was flipped over, onto his back, and the hand still holding a weapon was stepped on.

Crushed like his bones were nothing, the Bigfoot living up to his name.

Karl screamed as his arm disintegrated under the sheer mass of the creature.

The pain was excruciating.

Bigfoot roared.

Karl screamed again.

Bigfoot waved his massive arm low, the claws cleanly slicing through Karl's neck.

CHAPTER TWENTY-SEVEN

"Whatever it was, I think it's gone," Buck said. It was getting lighter outside, which was good. He wasn't fooling anyone, though. He knew exactly what had been out there.

If we can hold out for another hour or so, we might have a chance, Buck thought.

Mario was done with the bags. They each had two of them, filled with water bottles and various snacks. Not enough if they wanted to survive for longer than a few days, but the unspoken thought was the same for all three: if they needed to stay on the mountain longer than that, chances are they'd be dead.

The screams had stopped, which was either good or bad. With any luck, the Bigfoot would be busy dragging the dead up to its lair and not hunting for anyone left.

"We can get to the trikes and get down to where the vehicles are hidden within half an hour," Mario said. "Any trail going down the mountain will lead us to the road, too. If you think you're lost just stay on a path and it will dump out to the bottom."

"We'll follow you," Aiden said.

They waited ninety more minutes until it was definitely light enough outside. No sense in trying in the dark. Buck had mentioned Bigfoot lived in a cave and could likely see in the dark, so they wanted to even it out.

No sense in Bigfoot having yet another advantage over them.

Mario was out the back door first, followed by Aiden and Buck guarding their six. He had his bags and a weapon in hand and remembered the time they'd played paintball. How much fun it was pretending they were Army men.

This was not even remotely fun. Buck kept his eye behind them, but so far nothing stirred.

Mario groaned and Buck saw what he was groaning about.

Five men had been gutted and their body parts strewn about the weeds and dirt, the looks of pain and surprise etched on what was left of their faces.

So much death, Buck thought. There might be a hundred workers in camp. He wondered if they were the last three alive, and if Bigfoot was searching for them. He might be watching right now, toying with his last three victims.

"Pick up the pace," Mario said.

Buck could see the open garage where the trikes were stored. Even with the two they'd left on the top of the mountain, there were more than enough to ride.

"Bigfoot didn't destroy them," Mario said, sounding relieved. He opened the wall case and took out three sets of keys. They were all numbered.

"Time to ride or die," Aiden said. He took a set of keys from Mario and found the right three-wheeler.

Buck and Mario were ready now, all three ready to start their engines and take off.

Mario started his engine. "Follow me."

All three took off out of the garage, aiming for the road leading into the camp. Exiting to hopeful freedom.

Buck nearly stopped, paralyzed, when he saw two Bigfoot heading in their direction.

Two? No. This can't be, Buck thought.

Unfortunately, he was wrong. There were at least six he could now see, and they were beginning to surround them.

Mario screamed and took off.

He got to the start of the road before a Bigfoot swiped at him, slicing off Mario's head with its claws, like it was nothing.

Buck took off, heading toward a smaller trail behind the garage, with Aiden following.

Don't panic. You can do this. Time to go home and stay alive. Time to not stop until there is no trail left, Buck thought.

Aiden was right behind him but so was a Bigfoot. Maybe more than one.

Buck was bouncing up and down as he gunned the trike, giving what was left of Mario a glance and then looking away. Buck gripped the trike as he puked over his shoulder, hoping he wasn't covering Aiden with it.

Gross, Buck thought. If they survived this he hoped Aiden would punch him for it. That would mean they both survived.

Buck shot across a small field of weeds and found the main trail coming up, big enough for a car. The bosses had driven up in an SUV but Buck knew it had either been torn apart or the Bigfoot group would destroy it if they tried to drive down the mountain.

Trees were falling on either side of them. At least one Bigfoot was keeping pace with them.

Buck realized how lucky they'd been, wandering around the cave system. There could be a lot of the creatures living in the caves. What if they'd walked into a large cave and it was filled with them?

We'd be dead already, Buck thought.

Buck started to see vehicles parked under trees and covered by branches and tarps. He had no idea where they'd parked the van, though.

He slowed just enough for Aiden to get next to him. "Where's the van?"

Aiden took the lead.

Buck caught a glimpse of a Bigfoot behind them, coming down the trail.

More than one. I can't wrap my head around it, Buck thought. He supposed it made sense. How else would there be Bigfoot if there weren't initially a male and a female? Like the chicken and the egg idea, he guessed.

He wanted to shut up his stupid thoughts and focus on getting to the van, off the trike and into the van before getting killed.

Aiden stopped his three-wheeler and jumped off, slamming against his van; he was moving so fast.

As Buck pulled over, he saw a Bigfoot coming around the side of the van.

Another came over the top, crushing the roof in.

Buck started his engine again as Aiden was pulled onto the top of what was left of his van.

No. No, Buck thought, unable to scream. Stunned into silence.

It was over quickly for Aiden, who had his head twisted right off his body, while the Bigfoot on the ground bit into his left leg.

Another three Bigfoot were running at Buck, who spun out on the trike and took off.

He got about fifty feet before a giant arm swiped at him and Buck overcorrected, the trike falling to his left.

A thick sharp nail sliced his throat open.

The trike went right over the side of a ditch and began rolling, taking Buck with it.

Buck was unable to scream because his throat was a flayed mass of flesh, and he could no longer feel anything in his legs.

CHAPTER TWENTY-EIGHT

The official story was simple: a rival criminal group had swept in and killed everyone at the camp. Once the government had gone through and identified everyone, there were nearly one hundred dead.

Buck was the only survivor. The police came to talk to him, but it was no use.

His throat had been slashed to strips and his vocal cords severed. Both of his legs had been shattered from the fall. If he'd been higher up the mountain with a tumble like he'd had he'd be dead.

The doctors told him he'd never walk again. He'd been paralyzed and only his broken arms would heal enough for him to use them, to be able to write again.

His parents stayed at the hospital and kept the television on, watching live coverage of the massacre.

No mention of Bigfoot. Ever. Not on the news, not in the papers, not online.

In time, Buck healed enough to leave the hospital. He'd never walk or talk again.

He often had nightmares about Bigfoot tracking his scent and crashing into his bedroom.

Buck often thought about the basketball-sized lump of gold still in the caves.

He'd never be able to go back up the mountain, and knew telling anyone would be inviting their death.

Buck knew the monsters were still up there, too.

THE END

Check out other great

Cryptid Novels!

P.K. Hawkins

THE CRYPTID FILES

Fresh out of the academy with top marks, Agent Bradley Tennyson is expecting to have the pick of cases and investigations throughout the country. So he's shocked when instead he is assigned as the new partner to "The Crag," an agent well past his prime. He thinks the assignment is a punishment. It's anything but. Agent George Crag has been doing this job for far longer than most, and he knows what skeletons his bosses have in the closet and where the bodies are buried. He has pretty much free reign to pick his cases, and he knows exactly which one he wants to use to break in his new young partner: the disappearance and murder of a couple of college kids in a remote mountain town. Tennyson doesn't realize it, but Crag is about to introduce him to a world he never believed existed: The Cryptid Files, a world of strange monsters roaming in the night. Because these murders have been going on for a long time, and evidence is mounting that the murderer may just in fact be the legendary Bigfoot.

Gerry Griffiths

DOWN FROM BEAST MOUNTAIN

A beast with a grudge has come down from the mountain to terrorize the townsfolk of Porterville. The once sleepy town is suddenly wide awake. Sheriff Abel McGuire and game warden Grant Tanner frantically investigate one brutal slaying after another as they follow the blood trail they hope will eventually lead to the monstrous killer. But they better hurry and stop the carnage before the census taker has to come out and change the population sign on the edge of town to ZERO.

Check out other great
Cryptid Novels!

Hunter Shea
LOCH NESS REVENGE

Deep in the murky waters of Loch Ness, the creature known as Nessie has returned. Twins Natalie and Austin McQueen watched in horror as their parents were devoured by the world's most infamous lake monster. Two decades later, it's their turn to hunt the legend. But what lurks in the Loch is not what they expected. Nessie is devouring everything in and around the Loch, and it's not alone. Hell has come to the Scottish Highlands. In a fierce battle between man and monster, the world may never be the same. Praise for THEY RISE : "Outrageous, balls to the wall...made me yearn for 3D glasses and a tub of popcorn, extra butter!" – The Eyes of Madness "A fast-paced, gore-heavy splatter fest of sharksploitation." The Werd "A rocket paced horror story. I enjoyed the hell out of this book." Shotgun Logic Reviews

BAKER COUNTY
BIGFOOT
CHRONICLE

C.G. Mosley
BAKER COUNTY BIGFOOT CHRONICLE

Marie Bledsoe only wants her missing brother Kurt back. She'll stop at nothing to make it happen and, with the help of Kurt's friend Tony, along with Sheriff Ray Cochran, Marie embarks on a terrifying journey deep into the belly of the mysterious Walker Laboratory to find him. However, what she and her companions find lurking in the laboratory basement is beyond comprehension. There are cryptids from the forest being held captive there and something...else. Enjoy this suspenseful tale from the mind of C.G. Mosley, author of Wood Ape. Welcome back to Baker County, a place where monsters do lurk in the night!

 SEVERED**PRESS**

Check out other great

Cryptid Novels!

Ian Faulkner

CRYPTID

Be careful what you look for. You might just find it.1996. A group of 14 students walked into the trackless virgin forests of Graham Island, British Columbia for a three-day hike. They were never seen again. 2019. An American TV crew retrace those students' steps to attempt to solve a 23-year-old mystery.A disparate collection of characters arrives on the island. But all is not as it seems. Two of them carry dark secrets. Terrible knowledge that will mean death for some – but a fighting chance of survival for others. In the hidden depths of the forests – man is on the menu. Some mysteries should remain unsolved...

Eric S. Brown

LOCH NESS HORROR

The Order of the Eternal Light, a secret organization have foretold the end of the human race. In order to save all humanity, agents of the Order must locate the Loch Ness Monster and obtain a sample of its blood for within in it is the key to stopping the apocalypse but finding the monster will be no easy task.